WHEN DEATH'S AWAY

ON BEHALF OF DEATH, BOOK 4

E.G. STONE

TARNEY BRAE CREATIVE ENDEAVOURS

Copyright © 2021 by E.G. Stone

A Tarney Brae Creative Endeavours Production

Cover design by Fay Lane

Edits by Michael Evan

All rights reserved.

No part of this book may be reproduced in any form or by any electronic or mechanical means, including information storage and retrieval systems, without written permission from the author, except for the use of brief quotations in a book review.

❀ Created with Vellum

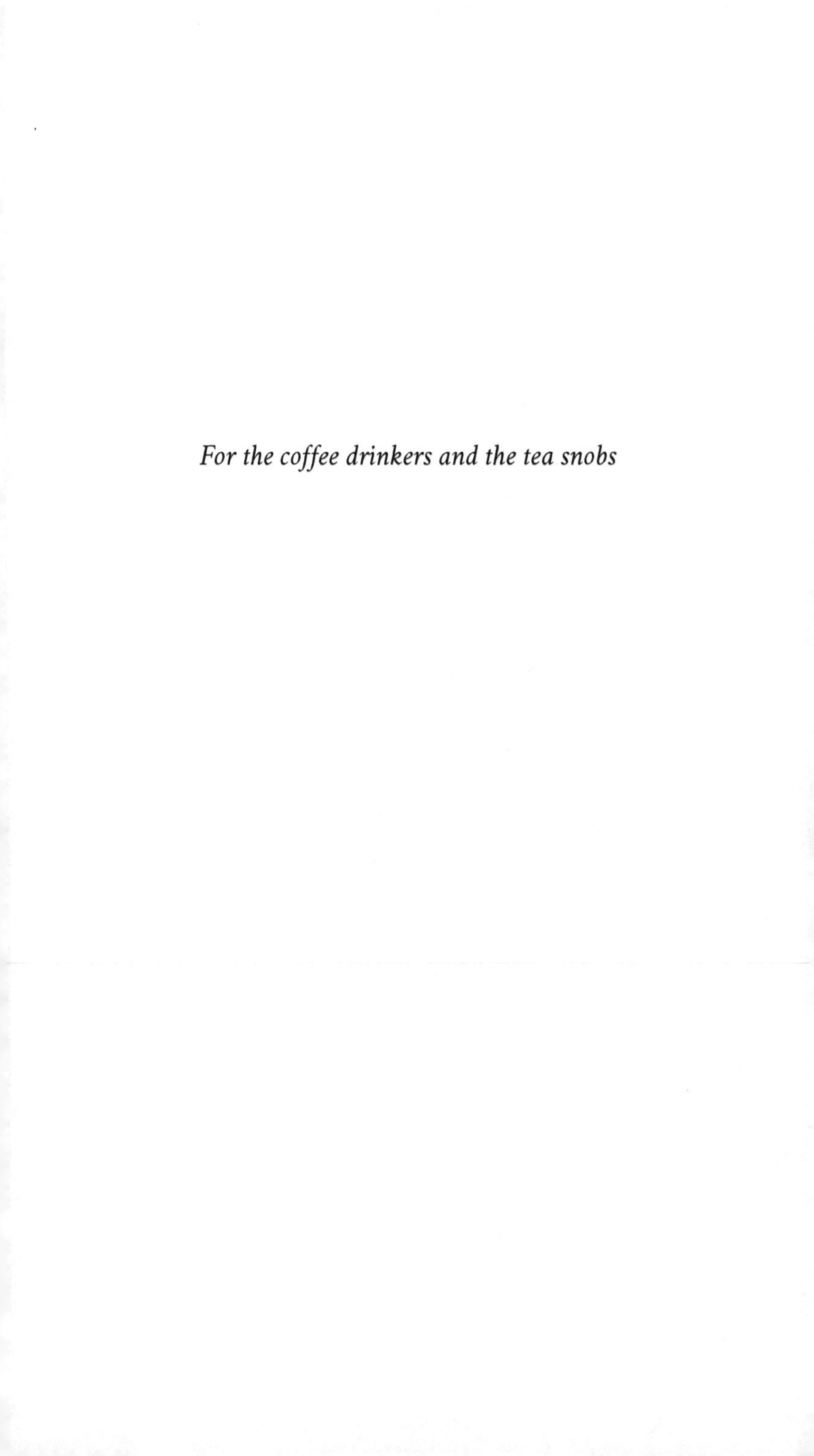

For the coffee drinkers and the tea snobs

VACATION FOR DEATH

I discovered that preparing for dinner with a djinn while also experiencing "phantom soul syndrome" was like an exercise in herding cats, while blind, with catnip smeared all over. Essentially, it was more or less a disaster.

My name is Cal Thorpe, I work for Death, and honestly, things are as confusing as they seem.

Neja was a djinn with whom I had struck a bargain about a week ago to have dinner. In exchange for helping me undo a death curse, I would invite her over to dinner. Of course, the wish had gone terribly wrong and we had accidentally released Al Capone on the streets of Modern day Chicago, but it all had worked out. Mostly. Now it was my turn to fulfil my end of the bargain. Initially, I thought it was meant to be some sort of date, but things went wonky as they were wont to do, and I was left entirely unsure as to whether or not she was actually interested in me, whether I was fulfilling some sort of weird elsewhere bargain, or if I had just misunderstood the entire situation. The logical part of my personality that took over when my emotions were nonfunctional decided that it was even odds to any of the options.

The hard part, though, was not determining the motives behind Neja's scheduled dinner, but sorting through my ever shifting emotions and thoughts to try and concentrate long enough to actually cook food. See, Death had lost my soul a while back, and the temporary arrangement in which I borrowed Al Capone's soul so that I wouldn't become an emotionless zombie or some sort of psychopath or hyperrational Vulcan had failed. Badly. However, as a result of some strange connection with Al Capone's soul, I was experiencing what Death called "phantom soul syndrome." This basically meant that I would occasionally feel surges of emotion that would make things seem almost, well, normal certainly wasn't the right word. These brief moments of emotional activity were usually very strong and unpredictable. But they kept me close enough to human that I wasn't going to fall into any of the traps that being soulless might cause.

It also meant that I had a strange obsession with very simple things. Coffee was a sure bet to making me experience ecstatic joy. Spoons had become the bane of my existence. And I was absolutely fascinated by the camera on my phone, which resulted in me taking rather a lot of pictures and then subsequently posting them on social media for all of Elsewhere to peruse. My series on my shoes had got quite a lot of interest.

The rest of the time, I was more or less apathetic

about things. Though, I will admit to a few introspective moments in the middle of the night when I realised that my existence was a strange one. Very strange.

Then again, I shouldn't have expected any different considering that I was Death's marketing agent. One must expect a certain amount of strangeness when working for Death.

The doorbell rang and I paused for a moment, considering the sound. It occurred to me that I hadn't actually ever heard my doorbell ringing before. I lived in a building that was both home and office. The office occupied the bottom floor of the old world style building, made of stone and ivy. The interior of my office was thoroughly modern, excepting the desks for myself, Yolanda my assistant, and Agravane a junior marketing agent with my firm. My living space occupied the rest of the building, and it was anything but modern. Death had furnished it with belongings from my old home in the mortal realms and then added a few extra pieces. The result was something between truly elegant leather and wood furnishings and eclectic comfort. I had bookshelves along the walls, a large television sitting before a massive sprawling sofa, rugs on the wood floors, pictures from my past life on one wall and photographs from my new life on another. It was a wonderful space, in my estimation, even considering the lack of emotional connection I felt to it at the moment. But I had never actually heard the doorbell ring. That struck me as odd. Was I really that isolated? Did I really have no one to invite over?

The doorbell rang again and I blinked.

"Uh, Cal?" Yolanda stuck her head out from the kitchen where she had been helping me prepare food. She had offered her services after my first attempt had made the entire building smell like burnt toast. She was wearing an apron covered in yellow duckies that she had stolen from me. It didn't quite fit her rock troll frame, but I wasn't going to say anything. Not when she was helping me with cooking. "Maybe you should go answer the door?"

"Yes, I should go answer the door." I turned and walked to the door, opening the solid hickory slab and rather thought my jaw should drop at the sight that met me. Since it was just a thought, not an actual motion, I just put on a theoretically pleasant smile. "I believe that you look quite good."

Neja smirked. She was not tall, as you saw with most immortal or magical beings in Elsewhere, but she was possessed of that same immortal grace and elegance. She was well muscled, with blue grey skin and silvery white hair that was, at the moment, tucked up with a pair of chopsticks. She wore, instead of the sleeveless jumpsuit that I had first seen her in, a pair of full leather leggings and a flowy black shirt. She didn't wait for me to invite her in, which was good since I didn't think that I was emotionally capable enough to consider such a politeness. She took in my living space, turning around in a neat circle, and nodded.

"Nice digs," she said. There was something hesitant in her voice that told me perhaps she was uncomfortable or uncertain of what should happen next. To be fair, I was also uncertain as to what should happen next, but that was partly because I was not entirely certain what the event for tonight was.

"Before I invite you in to eat, I wish to ask for clarifications that I may understand the appropriate way to act for this evening. Is this a fulfillment of an obligation? Or was this meant to be more along the lines of a date? Understanding the answer to that question will allow me to act more appropriately. Your hair smells nice." The last statement surprised me a little, but not hugely. Impulse control was currently not my best ability. Emotions and thoughts sprang into my head like flashes of lightning, and there was nothing the logical side of me could do to stop them.

"I'm sorry, what?" This time, she did not wince, she smiled. I found that sight to be sufficiently distracting enough that I didn't answer her question.

Yolanda shuffled out from the kitchen, wiping her hands on the yellow ducky apron. Her greenish skin was smeared with a little sauce right above her left cheek bone, but she did not seem to notice. She shuffled over and bobbled her head at Neja. "You are the djinn who helped save Cal in Chicago."

"Well, if he were acting normally, I'm not sure Cal would agree that I saved him. But I will accept that explanation. I'm Neja." Neja held out her hand for Yolanda to shake, and my assistant took it gladly. In fact, Yolanda was fairly beaming. As she was generally a cheerful sort, I did not attribute any special significance to this.

"I am Yolanda. Cal is my boss. And no, he is not

acting normally. His unusualness has got a bit worse. He lost his soul, which you well know, and now he is experiencing strange bouts of emotional episodes interspersed with apathetic, logical episodes. If you wish to get him interested in the conversation, you should discuss coffee."

I ignored Yolanda's hand placed sympathetically on my shoulder and instead seized upon the most wonderful substance in the world. "I got this new coffee from the Yucatán, imported from the mortal realms, and it is roasted to perfection. There's just a hint of cinnamon in it, but enough robustness to really get you going in the morning. Agravane told me that there was a coffee growing enclave somewhere in Elsewhere, but he refuses to tell me where for fear that I will go there and demand to not only taste everything but also possibly move there. I think that might not be such a bad idea, actually as—"

Neja put a hand over my mouth, effectively stopping my discussion of the most wonderful substance in the world. "Yeah, we won't be discussing that. Are the symptoms getting at all clear? Are they telling you where his soul is?"

Yolanda shook her head. "No, not even Death can find his soul right now. It remains a mystery. Now," Yolanda said with a flourish, clapping her hands together, "I am going to pull the pot roast out of the oven and you can enjoy your dinner."

"Great. Thank you." Neja turned to me and twined her arm through mine, leading me over to the first bookshelf. "How about a tour?"

"I can provide you with all of the pertinent information in the form of the tour. However, I feel that I should perhaps ask once again for further clarification on what the expectations for this evening are, so that I can act appropriately." The joy that had come with the discussion of coffee was now replaced by something more calm, steady. It wasn't quite pure hyper-rationality, nor was it distinct interest. It was just a smoothness that was mildly relieving from the roller coaster of the day's emotions. Neja patted my arm and turned her attention to the books, the first shelf being nonfiction memoirs and biographies, as well as some discussions on the theoretical principles of time, acquired after my run in with that very being. None of them quite captured his essence.

"If it were anybody else, I would say you're trying to take the mystery out of things. But, it would be my lot to be interested in someone who physically cannot be interested back. At least not yet. How about this: we get through tonight by having pleasant conversation over Yolanda's pot roast, and then we reevaluate the potential implications of a relationship some time in the future."

Neja plucked a discussion of Socrates from the shelf and did not meet my gaze. I took a moment to consider, trying to understand what it was that her words actually meant.

"You wish to date me, but not as my current self? Is it because of my lack of emotional response?" The larger part of me simply sought to understand, while a smaller part flinched away in hurt. Objectively speaking, Neja was the first female of any sort that I had, well, dated for lack of a better word, since about two years before entering into the service of Death. I knew that my life now stretched almost endlessly before me as I was an immortal, but there was a tug of... loneliness, perhaps, that pulled at me at Neja's words.

"I simply think you need to get a handle on things before trying to invest yourself into something else," Neja said. She replaced the book and looked at me with disinterest in her eyes. The smile she wore was polite. "Now, tell me Cal, how has your training with Agravane been progressing? I believe he promised to whip you into shape so that you might defend yourself against any future attacks. I mean, just because you can't die doesn't mean that you shouldn't be able to defend yourself, right?"

The brief touch of loneliness or sadness or whatever it was that tightened my throat vanished. I launched into a discussion of the logical merits of learning to defend myself, as well as a discussion of my previous physical exercise experiences, why it was that I was currently having difficulties reconciling my level of capability with that which Agravane demanded of me, as well as a discussion of various ways that humans were naturally much weaker than many of the beings in Elsewhere.

This discussion, and Neja's input on weaponry and various forms of martial arts, lasted throughout dinner. I did not have time to dwell on what my various emotional responses meant, nor did I feel another surge, though I did avoid my spoon studiously.

By the time Neja left, I felt that I had performed sufficiently well in my dinner host capacity. We mentioned the possibility of seeing each other soon, shook hands, and then she laughed. The door clicked closed behind her and I felt a momentary shortness of breath, and an urge to sigh, neither of which made logical sense. I turned and trudged over to my couch, sitting and experiencing immediate relief as my muscles relaxed.

"How was your dinner?"

I lifted my head and looked at Death, his sudden and impossible appearance doing absolutely nothing to surprise me. I'd had three days of simply settling down back to my normal marketing work, despite the fact that he had promised to speak with me about a holiday of some sort. I'd known that we would be having a conversation soon. I also knew that Death could appear wherever he wished, and that, generally speaking, the respect for his people's privacy kept him from doing just that. However, Death was also aware that I did not particularly have any emotional investment in whether or not my lodgings were private at the moment, so the fact that he had appeared there was not entirely unexpected. Also, he had a previous habit of expressing curiosity in things, so coming to ask me about my evening with the djinn fit perfectly.

Mostly, though, I did not currently have the capacity to be surprised.

"I believe she was, how do you say, testing the waters as it were. She seemed interested in potentially pursuing a relationship with me, but not in my current state of being. As a result, we discussed my training with Agravane in self-defence matters, and she went on her way." I lay my head back on the arm of the couch.

"I'm sorry. I imagine it would be considerably different if you had a soul. Many immortal beings do not have one and do not understand why it is that humans require them. I believe our djinn should be truly intrigued by you. But, she is also a slave to her nature and will go where the desire lives." Death's voice didn't sound sympathetic, but his words did sort of provide comfort. Or at least, they would not have provided comfort had I been in a position to receive comfort.

"I imagine she and I will cross paths again in the future. As it stands currently, my most logical course of action would be to continue to work here and to train with Agravane, while also searching for clues as to the whereabouts of my soul. On a related note, do you think that the unevenness in my emotions will smooth out?" I lifted my head to look at Death, taking in his impeccably tailored pinstripe three-piece suit, the pocket square, today a pale lavender that matched the sprig tucked into his buttonhole. He lifted a hand, blacker than night and wreathed in shadow, the digits thin and capable. He wobbled it side to side, a nonverbal expression of "so-so".

"This is all quite new to me. I do not know whether or not your motions will stabilise, as you are not currently with your soul, nor are you growing a new one as it were. You are experiencing the memory of something that is no longer there. It is possible it will fade again, but I'm unsure. However, that is not why I came to see you tonight, nor is your dinner with Neja the reason. The state of your relationships has no bearing on the current situation. It is, in fact, your soullessness that I require."

Seized by sudden curiosity, I scrambled to a sitting position and stared wide-eyed at Death. My mouth hung open and I ran through the possibilities of what that statement might mean. Death chuckled at my obvious interest, the sound only piquing my curiosity more. The sensation floated through me, tingling in my veins and making my mouth dry in anticipation.

"I am going on holiday, and I need someone to... fill in for me while I am gone."

Death stared at me, the voids that were his eyes seeming to shimmer with some hidden light, a strange humour flashing there for a moment. It took me a few seconds, coming off of the emotional rush as I was, to understand the logical implications of his words.

Death was going on holiday. And he needed me to act for him while he was gone. He wanted me to be Death. Oh yes, this would end spectacularly.

I burst out laughing.

DEATH TAKES A HOLIDAY

*I*t took longer than it should have for me to stop laughing. By the time I had got whatever emotion that was under control, my eyes were watering and my belly was sore. I straightened up on the couch and wiped the moisture from my eyes, replacing my glasses on my nose.

"I apologise about that, but apparently I found it to be a rather and amusing suggestion." I blinked and looked at Death, waiting for him to say something about how it had simply been a test condition, an attempt to see whether or not my emotional responses were spontaneous or to do with familiar things, like coffee. Oh, coffee, how I long for it. Slightly bitter tasting on my tongue, the heat filled me with caffeine—

"I assure you, I was not making a joke. I am quite serious." Death tilted his head to watch me, but I didn't exhibit anymore unusual emotional responses. I did, however, exhibit a certain amount of technical confusion at the statement. I waited for Death to explain. He took a breath and shook his head, letting it out slowly. It was a weary sigh, one born from eons of dealing with beings who could not even fully understand him. Or perhaps that was a part of me trying something on to him that he did not feel. I much preferred to stick to known facts.

"As you know, Life and I are often at odds. Some many centuries ago, we both wished to… take a holiday as it were, at the same time. It did not end well. The town of Pompeii was never quite the same."

Right, because accidentally setting off a volcano was something to discuss, as though it were a perfectly ordinary event on a holiday. I continued to stay silent. Death watched me, as if waiting for a response, as if expecting some sort of indignant shock or horror at the fact that he and Life were powerful enough to cause such immense destruction. This was not new information.

"We had to come to an agreement never to take our holiday at the same time. This year is my turn. I have precisely ten days on a beach in the Virgin Islands and I intend to enjoy them. However, it also means I must appoint a proxy in my absence. As a human with a soul would be too incompatible, I usually look to one of the beings of Elsewhere. However, they are also too distantly connected, too keenly aware of the power that being my proxy holds. I much prefer to appoint someone whom I can trust."

"Such a statement indicates that you, therefore, trust me." That made logical sense, but there were still pieces of this situation I did not fully understand. Such as what it was exactly I was meant to do for Death. Was I meant to kill people? That did not seem like something I would be terribly good at, even if I were ruled purely by logic rather than emotion. I was, after all, still human, and many of the human instincts and logic told us that the greatest number of people surviving was best for the species. I could perhaps override such evolutionary notions if I took into account the fact that I was employed by Death and therefore had an obligation to him to do what was demanded of me, but I was not entirely sure that such thinking would prevail for long.

There was the fact that I was simply not as powerful as Death. Surely many hundreds of thousands of people were dying every moment of every day, and that was simply in the mortal realms. I did not know what would happen in Elsewhere, how many of the magical beings were mortal or whether their mortal lives were ended. I could not physically be in all of those places at once. Not to mention I didn't actually know how Death went about doing whatever it was he did. Did he kill people? Did he sever their souls? He had once told me he was a facilitator rather than a murderer, closer to a ferryman than a killer. But he had also said that his business was not involved in whatever came after. I had only witnessed Death act in his official capacity on one occasion, when he had to kill Justice, the aurai who went mad with love for Life. And even then, I hadn't fully understood what was going on.

"Perhaps you had better say something before your expression fractures, Cal," Death said, reaching out and patting me on the shoulder as if I were choking. The act did manage to break me out of my particular meditative state. I heaved a deep breath, my lungs feeling starved for oxygen. I wasn't sure if that was part of this phantom soul business or if I had actually held my breath.

"I think you're going to have to leave detailed instructions for me," was all that I managed to say. All of my questions would take hours to go through, and I very much doubted that Death wanted to delay his holiday to get into a potentially philosophical discussion with an emotional robot. An emotionally unstable robot. Besides, I doubted Death wanted to reveal all of his secrets to me anyways. Even if I was going to be acting as his proxy.

"I will. I can perhaps anticipate some of your more immediate question and answer them now, but I will be certain to leave detailed instructions on what you are to do tomorrow. The first: I do not have a book or a ledger with people's names in it, telling me when their time is up, nor do I keep a room of hour glasses stretching to infinity. It is all instinct and feeling, a cry let out by the soul as its body fails. I am called to the time when the physical and the metaphysical no longer exist within the same space. I will not be able to transfer all of that feeling, that instinct to you, but I can provide you with a similar spell so that you know where to go. And as for what you will be doing, many of the finer aspects of my role in the universe cannot be understood by you. People will be terrified of you. Or they will be pleased to see you. Some will greet you, and some will never even know that you were there. Your job is not to comfort, nor to explain, not to converse or defend, yours is simply to remove them, to separate the ties that bind. What comes after that, I cannot say, but you will not be able to take them to the point where they go beyond. For now, you will merely sever the soul from the body and collect them in an orb. I will deal with it once I return."

Collect the souls that I was to sever in and orb based on a feeling given to me by a magical spell. It seemed simple enough. At this point, the rest of Death's explanation had made things more confusing than otherwise. I decided to ignore it completely and instead focus on the tangible things that I could do. It was at this point in my logical analysis of the facts that my emotions began to rear their ugly head.

The first thing I felt: panic. How was I to sever a being's soul? Use a scythe? Was I about to touch them as Death did? How would I go to every single one who needed it when I was still one person who could only be in one place at one time? I started breathing heavily, feeling as I had the first time I met Death, when he found me in a park told me that everything I thought was real was not, and what I thought was not real was, when he offered me a job to work for him. I took my head and placed it between my knees, trying to get control of my breathing.

Death patted my shoulder awkwardly. I took a few seconds to get my breathing under control and after that, the panic that I felt simply fell away. I straightened in the chair and looked at Death.

"I wouldn't worry too much about the details. You will figure this out, I am sure. Instinct will take you far. And as for the rest, it is perhaps better that they should remain mysteries." The last was said with a slight smirk, a knowledge that he held that no one else ever would, done with a twinkle in his void eyes. Had I been feeling things at that very moment instead of feeling nothing, I would've perhaps been worried at such an obvious display of power. As it was, I took Death at his word.

"A brief question, to perhaps assuage my curiosity?" I folded my hands neatly together and tilted my head at Death. He nodded imperiously. "What do you do on holiday? On holiday? Surely you don't just sit around drinking martinis or whatever while reading a book? Or take a tour bus to volcanoes. It seems rather unusual things for a truly immortal being such as yourself."

Death chuckled, standing and re-buttoning his suit jacket. He brushed his hands over the fabric, smoothing the lines, and then turned back to me with a nod. "At precisely seven in the morning tomorrow, be at my offices so that the transfer of power can take place. I trust you will do nothing that I would not do while I am away. Try to keep the place in one piece."

I nodded. I was meant to go out collecting souls. Then it shouldn't have been that much of a worry to keep Death's manor house in one piece. Logically speaking, I would probably not be spending much of my time here. Ten days. Let my instinct guide me. Collect souls into an orb. I should be able to manage that. After all, I had travelled through time, dealt with a semi-reincarnated American gangster, even solved the murder that hadn't been committed by Death. Truly, I could handle such a relatively simple task. Something in the back of my mind told me, though, that it would indeed be a simple task, but not an easy one.

Death didn't offer any more words, either of advice or warning. He simply strode to the door, graceful as ever and as powerful as, well, Death. No one would ever mistake him for a tourist on holiday, no matter where he went.

With Death gone, my date night with Neja turned into who knows what, and Yolanda likely down of the offices catching up on some Netflix, my living quarters seemed very empty. This was not a logical emotion, nor was it one that brought about a surge of feeling. It was simply an assertion made by my mind. It did not make sense. And yet it was.

As it did not seem to be related to my strange bouts of unstable emotion, I put it from my mind by doing the dishes. Logically, they needed to be done. If I did not do them now, then any food particles left on them would harden overnight and cleaning them the next day would be far more difficult. Also, the rhythmic motions of rinsing the dishes and putting them into the dishwasher, of putting leftovers into the fridge—though I knew Agravane and Yolanda would manage to sneak in here and steal them at some point—all of these things calmed my mind. Huh. I had not known that it needed to be calmed.

Death's assignment must have shocked me more

thoroughly than any of the events preceding had done. This emotional disturbance had lasted longer than any of the others I had experienced thus far, excepting one incident where Agravane and Yolanda accidentally let me ramble on about coffee for nearly an hour simply because they didn't know what was wrong with me. But this was different. It endured. Even as I went and prepared for bed, brushing my teeth and cleaning my glasses as I placed them on the bedside table, it persisted. I turned off the light and closed my eyes, fully expecting to drop off to sleep as logically as I knew I should.

I did not sleep at all.

Morning found me feeling nothing, as was normal. I was, however, physically experiencing the effects of having little sleep and several unusual emotional experiences the evening before. Breakfast was a simple affair, me running through the motions of eating toast and eggs and ignoring a cup of coffee since I knew, logically that I did not have time for expounding on its virtues and savouring its magnificent flavours, as I had to meet Death in his office. At 6:50, I gathered my strength and walked over to Death's office, feeling more tired than I would care to admit, despite the influx of energy from my food.

When I stepped into Death's study, the old style club chairs and walls of books surrounding the fireplace a familiar sight, Death was standing there in the most unusual set of clothing. He wore a linen suit reminiscent of English tourists to Egypt in the 1920s and 30s, his necktie a flowered affair in a red silk. He had a straw hat on his head and light brown leather shoes on his feet, completely different from the standard black that I had seen him wear for so long. There were two leather suitcases near the door, fairly beat-up and obviously well used. Death greeted me with a smile, the lightness of his clothes contrasting greatly with the utter blackness that was the rest of him, shadows still reeling about him as though his magic were just too powerful to contain. For all I knew, it was.

"Good morning, Cal," Death greeted, sounding unusually cheerful. "You look as though you haven't slept."

I rubbed my eyes, feeling as though I had some grit left over from my sleepless nights stuck there. I yawned and replaced my glasses a moment later. "I didn't."

"Interesting. I would have thought that your natural tendency towards true apathy would've allowed you to sleep as normal. I wonder if there isn't something more going on than this phantom soul syndrome. Alas, I haven't the time to look into it now. I am meant to be leaving shortly." Death glanced at his watch on his wrist, something I had never before seen him wear. A pocket watch, perhaps. But not her wristwatch, like any other garish tourist wanted to know when their flight was. This was bizarre, and even more so that I noted it in my current hyperrational state of mind.

Death took a few steps towards me, holding out both his hands. I looked at them, wondering if I was meant to do something. "Take my hands, Cal. The transfer of power will begin," Death said, shaking his hands as though reminding me that they were there.

I reached out, my skin an inch away from his, before I felt compelled to speak. "I should perhaps remind you that the previous occasions on which you have made contact with me via skin to skin touch has not always ended well. I am fully aware that I cannot physically die, but are you quite certain that thi—"

"I am creating a conduit through which my power will flow. It is not a full transference of my power, nor am I going to affect your being as I have done before. This is… well, to be frank, it is something that is far too complicated for your limited mind to grasp. Trust me simply that it will work."

I studied Death's expression for a moment, wondering if it were somewhere between solemn and amused or if that was simply my imagination. In my current state, identifying other people's emotions was a skill at which I was not particularly adept. Still, even if I couldn't identify what Death was thinking or feeling, I did have to acknowledge that he was my boss and that I was meant to be obeying his orders. I reached out my hands, grasped his from above, and prepared to do my duty for the next ten days.

On three previous occasions, I have come into contact with Death's skin. The first was when he hired me and we shook hands. This replaced my life force, the thing that was keeping me mortal with my soul, which could not be killed. The second time was when we shook hands again, reversing that effect and instead replacing my life force with that of an immortal being.

The third time, Death touched me on the forehead and accidentally severed my soul, which was already separate from my body. Since I could not die, my soul disappeared and I was left in my current state. All three of those instances had been accompanied by bone shattering pain that left my veins on fire and my mind screaming in agony.

This was not like that at all.

For one, there was no pain. I felt power surging through me, testing the boundaries of my body as though a new person moving into an old house, seeing what was possible and what wasn't. It did not hurt, but did feel a bit as though my insides were being rearranged. Then, the flow of power increased, gathering together like a gravity well in the centre of my being, pulling in everything to me, as if the knowledge that all would come my way eventually was enough to sustain me, to make it as though I was the centring point in the universe and all else existed around me, inevitably drawn towards me. I was not the centre of the universe, I was not its purpose, I was simply its truth.

I felt the power reading around my skin and when I looked down, the shadows that had followed Death since the beginning of time were now writhing around me, their touch featherlight on my skin, an extension of my power.

And yet, it was not complete. This new magnificence that flowed through me, this power that soon became my very definition of being, it was not whole, not as it should be. The pieces that were missing were still contained in the being across from me, our hands touching. I knew, fully logically and without any emotion at all, that this impossible strength and power that was now mine was simply the lesser part of a greater whole. I was the truth of the universe, its full inevitability, and yet Death, standing before me, was more than that.

He released my hands a moment later and I let them fall to my sides, the shadows following them. "What an unusual sensation," I said, my voice strangely flat when all my logic told me that I should have been experiencing emotional instability just then.

"Indeed. I have left instructions on the desk. I shall see you in ten days' time." Death adjusted his hat and his necktie, strode over to where his suitcases waited, and then left his office as though he had never been there.

I lifted a hand and stared at it, my pale skin followed by a mist of living shadow. It was interesting to see the patterns that they followed, something close to Brownian chaos and yet not quite. The tugging at the centre of my being told me that I should go read the instructions before whatever this power was reared its head made me obey it unquestioningly.

A single sheet of paper was held down by an orb on a stand. These, I assumed, were my instructions and the vessel into which I was to collect souls. I picked up the orb, grabbed the sheet of paper, and was about to start reading when the door burst open and Life swanned in.

Something in the power within me was drawn to

her just as everything was drawn to me. The urge was so strong that I was standing before I even had time to blink. Life paused across the desk, looking at me with wide eyes of a colour that I never could quite pin down, her whole image one of ever-changing temptation and loveliness.

"Well, piffle," Life said, fisting a hand on her hip. "He's gone on holiday, hasn't he? I do wish he would tell me when these things are going to happen. It's not like I remember. Oh, well, so be it. Cal Thorpe, I require your assistance."

didn't really have any prior knowledge to know how to deal with Life demanding my assistance, so I simply did what I thought Death would do in a similar circumstance. I waved her to the chair in front of the desk, leaned back and steepled my fingers, waiting. Life rolled her eyes and sank into the chair.

Life was, generally speaking, the sort of person who immediately livened a room, drawing your attention, demanding that you do so much more than notice her. She was a being whose appearance I could not accurately describe except to say that she was one of the most beautiful things I had ever seen, intrinsically appealing in a way that no one else ever had been. I couldn't tell you the colour of her hair, the shade of her eyes, the clothing that she wore, only that she was designed to stimulate certain neurons and chemicals in my brain to elicit a pleasurable response. She was also, objectively speaking, terrifying. In my current logical state, I was perhaps less tempted by her than usual, but I did still find it vaguely unsettling. This was probably due to the influx of chemicals that my brain was producing without any related emotional response.

Or, I was experiencing emotion and just didn't know how to define it.

"Trying to emulate Death, I see?" Life picked up a paperweight that was sitting on death's desk and rolled it around her hands.

"In point of fact, no. I simply have no logical basis for how to interact with you at the current time, so I drew on my experience with Death and applied his actions, as I am meant to be his proxy. I am not trying to emulate him, I am simply using a logical model for the current situation." I folded my hands in front of me on the desk, deciding that steepling them was perhaps too close to emulation.

Life took in a deep breath and heaved a sigh, her shoulders moving dramatically. "Oh stars, you're still having problems with your soul. I thought you were dealing with Capone or whoever it was had solved this particular issue."

"The situation with Capone went rather sideways when his overwhelming instinct to regain Life was crossed with a djinn's wish magic. I had to terminate my deal prematurely. And Death says I am experiencing what he calls 'phantom soul syndrome.'"

It did not follow any logical sense that Death hadn't explained my situation to Life. Given that Death didn't actually fully understand my situation—or at least that was what he told me—I assumed that he would collaborate with Life in order to provide a solution. That logic seemed to be faulty, because Life tossed back her head, her hair producing a pleasant scent, and laughed. The sound filled the room and made my ears echo. I scratched at the right one.

Life rolled her eyes at my movements. "My goodness, you're dull. Though, if you are experiencing instability with your lack of soul, then perhaps you are not as dull. Phantom soul syndrome indeed. Well, no matter. I have more important things to talk about at the moment. You are acting as Death's proxy, are you not?"

I nodded.

Life clapped her hands together. "Good. I need you to go collect someone's soul."

I nodded again. "This seems a rational request," I said, picking up my instructions and glancing over them, not really comprehending any of it. "Death said that I would be responsible for collecting several souls, that the instinct to go to them would arise and I would be able to gather a person's soul in an orb. The instructions are meant to tell me how, but as yet I have not felt any particular rise in instinct that would perhaps lead me to a person whose soul needed to be—"

"Okay, let's set some ground rules. I don't need to hear every logical progression of thought that goes on inside your head." Life leaned forward and gave me an intense look, which I am fairly certain I misinterpreted as interest. "I just need to know whether you're going to do this or not?"

"Yes," I said, "this is one of the duties that I was

assigned to perform in Death's absence. As such, I will accompany you to collect the soul of whoever it is."

In one swift movement, Life rose from her chair and her presence seemed to fill the room with a satisfied smugness that I recognised from my experience with Al Capone. I rose as well, grabbing the orb and putting it into my jacket pocket. I took the instructions and folded them, figuring I would read them after we had got to wherever it was that we were meant to go. Hopefully, the person I was meant to be meeting would behave while I took the time to determine precisely how to collect their soul.

Life held out her hand, her hair moving about her like a cloud, her clothes rustling in some impossibly intangible wind. "Well then, let us depart."

"Oh, yes, travel to the mortal realms. This was something that I had not considered. It would perhaps be useful to read through Death's instructions before we travel to the mortal realms to capture the soul. Unless the soul is in Elsewhere, in which case I should still perhaps remain and read the instructions as it would only be logical to know precisely what it is that I am meant to be doing when we arrive in—"

Life heaved another sigh, this one thoroughly annoyed. "Less talking, more doing." With that, she snatched my hand out of the air and we vanished.

I have travelled between places in many different ways. The most unpleasant was by far travel by wyvern, a sort of pseudo-airplane travel distinct to Elsewhere that was jostling on the stomach and completely open to the elements. Travelling to and from the mortal realms was fairly pleasant, when doing it by Death's means of transportation. He provided a seamless transition; you were in one place one moment and in another the next. The Taxman had simply exchanged one place for the interior of an IRS building, perhaps the most startling means of travel, but that was bureaucracy for you.

Life was something else entirely. I don't know if it was the fact that I possessed some of Death's powers, or if it was simply the gravitas that Life held, but I felt my breath stolen from my lungs, my heart beating impossibly fast, wind blowing over my skin. Had I been able to feel emotions at that particular moment, I imagine I would have been feeling everything that it was possible to feel, for what was Life if not feeling. As it was, I simply felt a little nauseous and had to close my eyes until the world stopped moving around me.

We were standing at the edge of a cliff, the ground beneath my feet green and lush, the edge of the cliff leading right into a vast drop to the ocean, smashing on the rocks below. The sky was crisp and blue, the air biting but not completely cold. It smelled of salt and grass and freshness. And amidst the roar of the wind and the crash of the waves, I heard a humming noise.

I looked around, disregarding Life at my side, standing with her arms crossed and a scowl on her face. I had turned almost a complete circle when I spotted the person who was humming. He was, by all accounts, an old man. He had a beard down to his chest, scraggly with time. His head was nearly bald, only a few wisps of white hair catching in the wind.

His tan face was lined from years out in the sun, and he wore old, well-made clothing that had seen just as much life as he had.

I didn't know where we were. Given that the man in front of us looked human, I assumed we were in the mortal realms, but we could have been in Elsewhere and he could have been a Faerie or a sprite or some sort of impossibly old creature. And yet, I didn't think that we were in Elsewhere. My suspicions were confirmed when the man started speaking in an accent that sounded Scottish mixed with Eastern Indian.

"I was wondering when you would show up again, my dear," the man said, touching his fingers to his four head and nodding at Life. She sniffed and lifted her chin. "Though, I did think that you were going to bring your husband, not some... well I don't actually know what you are."

"My name is Cal Thorpe, and I am currently acting as Death's proxy. If you are acquainted with Life, then I assume you are aware of what is to happen next?" I took a step towards the man and he backed up to the edge of the cliff, wagging his finger at me and laughing.

"Ah, ah, we wouldn't want to do that, now would we? Well, Cal Thorpe, proxy for Death, it is a pleasure to meet you. Has the lady explained to you precisely what it is that you are meant to be doing here?" His heels hung over the edge of the cliff, but he seemed completely unconcerned. This was odd, considering that if he were to step over the cliff, I assumed he would be releasing his soul into my possession, regardless.

"Life mentioned simply that I needed to collect a soul. You shall have to excuse me a moment while I read the instructions on how precisely to collect a soul. I do apologise if this causes any particular distress, but this is my first morning on the job and I have not yet had time to review paperwork." I pulled the orb out of my pocket and the instructions out of my jacket, holding the orb in my left hand and the instructions in my right.

I was about to start reading when the man started laughing again, this time a full belly laugh that came with such an absurd situation that you simply couldn't contain it. I blinked, tilting my head. This was an illogical response for such a situation. Granted, yes, Death's proxy not knowing precisely how to do his job was rather... unusual, but it did not seem any reason to laugh.

"Oh, you really don't have any idea what's going on here, do you? Where did you find him, Life? He is so... Unfeeling. I don't imagine he would be your first choice for such an assignment!" The man stepped away from the edge, walking towards me with assuredness in his stride. I noticed that his feet were bare, which struck me as a little odd. This made me frown as it was the second thing I had found odd about this man.

The man slung his arm around my shoulder and I will admit to jumping at the contact. I didn't have a chance to move away, as my hands were occupied with the orb and the instructions. The man spread his hands out, indicating the horizon before me.

"Do you see all of this?" He looked at me, the hair of

his beard brushing against my shoulder. I wanted to take a step back, to straighten my suit and put some distance between me and this man. Instead, he kept talking. "All of this is the most wonderful thing in the world. This is life, no not the being you see next to you, but true life, the place where you get to experience emotions and pain and happiness and logic and strangeness and all of the beauty that is humanity and the wonder that is nature. And I was so devoted to it, to the pursuit of life, to the enjoyment of life, that this magnificent lady that you see here found me one day. She offered to me the role of her champion, one who would fight to defend her and love her."

The man took a deep breath in through his nose, clapped me on the shoulder and took a step back. Something in his expression turned solemn. "I accepted. On one condition: that she allow me to continue to enjoy life, to experience everything that she, and this place, had to offer forever, until such time as I experienced one moment of boredom."

Life tsked, clicking her tongue against her teeth. She looked away from this man, whose name I still didn't know. "It was a fair deal, as every human experiences boredom at least once every year. I assumed that you would eke out any amount of wonder and excitement and then in a moment of peace, you would succumb and that would be that."

The man took another step back, his solemn expression deepening even as he smiled, showing off a row perfectly healthy teeth. "How were you to know that I would experience four hundred years of life with not one moment of boredom? And here you are, tired of me, ready to consign me to Death simply because *you* are bored with *me*."

The man turned on his heel to face me, his body cutting Life out of the conversation as easily as if she had been just a normal person, easy to dismiss. "And you, Cal Thorpe, proxy for Death. Do you think I haven't met Death in all of these years? I know how he works. I know that there is the call, that ringing in your very core, a tug at your soul that pulls you towards who it is that's meant to die. After all, Death is the inevitable, the centre that cannot hold. So I ask you, Cal Thorpe, do you feel any tug? Any ringing? A call? Or can poor old Samuel Phipps go on going on?"

"I was informed by Death that I would indeed feel a rise in my instincts when such time came to collect a person's soul, but one problem with that is I do not currently possess a soul, and so cannot feel a tug in mind if that is indeed the means by which I am to ascertain whose soul is to be collected. At the moment, I do not feel any particular pull towards you, but that could simply be because I do not have the mechanism with which to feel such a thing. However, that does not logically follow as Death would not have gone on holiday were he not certain that matters would be well in hand while he was gone, which suggests that there is some means not related to my soul that I am to use to determine such things." As my answer was neither yes, nor no, I shrugged and hoped that this Samuel Phipps could understand.

Instead, he turned back to Life, waving a skeptical finger at me. "Where did you find this one?"

"He is my husband's creature, a mistake as much as an experiment. He is some sort of marketing agent, as though that could make my husband's reputation any better." Life stepped closer to me and ran a hand down my arm, the touch of her skin through my shirt and suit jacket enough to bring a change in temperature to my forehead. An unusual reaction, but not entirely unexpected when it came to Life and her symptoms.

"If you will give me a moment, I shall read the instructions and we can ascertain whether or not something is wrong with me or whether the situation is that you are simply not yet called to die." I looked away from Samuel and ruffled through the papers in my hands, skipping over the initial introductory paragraph, moving past the nature of the orb, skimming over the article to do with Death's filing system—it wasn't entirely certain why he had included that in the instructions unless he meant me to do filing. I would have to see the state of his office before he got back from holiday, to be sure that I hadn't missed some sort of essential office task — moved past the discussion of the nature of Life and Death and finally found the section devoted to the instinctual pull.

"I found it!" I said, jabbing my finger at the papers which were now being pulled on by the wind. "According to this, there is meant to be a sort of ethereal glow about a person when their soul is ready to be collected. Death seems to have set this particular sign specifically to me as I do not have a soul and, therefore—"

I looked up at Samuel Phipps and blinked, pushing my glasses up my nose with the hand holding the orb. "Interesting. You were not glowing before, but you are now. I suppose that means that Life is correct, and your soul is to be collected."

Samuel paled, the lines in his skin seeming to grow ever more intense. He took a step back to the edge of the cliff, his bare feet hanging once more over the edge. The glow remained steady, a yellow nimbus surrounding his body. Next to me, Life crowed in triumph, pointing a victorious finger in his direction.

"I told you! Every human experiences boredom. Of course, in his current state, anyone would be bored by Cal Thorpe's ridiculous ramblings. But it proves my point Samuel Phipps! Your soul is forfeit," Life said. She lifted her chin and looked expectantly at me. It took me a moment to realise that she was waiting for me to perform whatever task it was that I was meant to do in order to collect Samuel Phipps's soul, but I hadn't yet got to that bit in the instruction manual.

"One moment, if you please. I must find the appropriate—"

Before I could even lower my gaze to look at the papers, Phipps let out a cry of rage and leapt backwards off the edge of the cliff, plummeting to the waters below. The yellow nimbus of light seemed to grow stronger, a beacon that I could see from any distance, drawing me to him. Even as that light grew stronger, I could see more appearing on the horizon, flickering at the corner of my vision, demanding my attention. But the point was that Phipps wasn't dead yet. Somehow—likely to do with his prolonged connection to Life—he had survived that fall and likely intended to keep on living until I could catch up with him.

"Do you know, Life, I think it might be prudent that you have a conversation with Death about your champions once he gets back from holiday. We have had rather a few incidents with them, haven't we?" I pushed my glasses up my nose and stuffed the orb back into my pocket. If I didn't know better, I would have said that my voice was laced with sarcasm, but as I wasn't currently feeling sarcastic that surely could not be the case. Or perhaps it was. It would be appropriate given the situation with Life at the moment.

She snarled at me, the look feral and furious. "Have you ever stopped to consider, Cal, that my problems with my champions have only ever happened when you're around?"

I folded the instructions and put them back into my pocket, figuring that now was perhaps not the best time to read them. Then, definitely feeling sarcastic, I smirked at Life. "I'm not an all-powerful being. I think it's probably you."

pparently, Life couldn't just transport us to wherever Samuel Phipps was at that moment. She didn't and have an intrinsic connection to people's souls like Death did. She was aware of all life, but people's continued and constant interactions with her made it impossible for her to find one soul. Personally, I thought that such an explanation didn't follow logic at all, as I had seen Life appear in many places without being called. I also knew that she had a special connection to Phipps considering that he was her champion. She hadn't said as much, but I got the impression that Life was stalling, simply because she was naturally opposed to Death, and now Phipps was marked. Before, it would have been easy to say that he wasn't marked, that he belonged in Life's domain and she would have complained rallied against him, but she would have accepted it and moved on.

That was just what Life did.

Phipps had got bored in the moments that I was

speaking, though, and therefore his agreement with Life expired. His soul glowed, drawing me in like a beacon.

I followed Life down the hill, reading the instructions as I went, ignoring her rambling. Walking and reading wasn't perhaps the best course of action, considering my ability to draw just about every sort of trouble my direction, but it was what was available. I needed to go tend to the glows, deal with the job that had been set for me. So I read, and I walked.

The instructions said the orb was a receptacle, a storage device. I needed only to release a person's soul and they would naturally be drawn to the storage device. I had to be present at the deaths of all the people, though my mere existence and presence would provide for such smaller deaths such as plants and animals. Their life-cycles were different; they rarely needed personal attention.

Great, very interesting, but how in the world was I actually meant to sever a person's soul?

"If Death hadn't been on holiday, none of this would have happened. We wouldn't have any crazed people running about, trying to escape you. Who knows what sort of damage Phipps will cause in the name of eking out a last few days moments of enjoyment before the inevitable happens. He knows it as well as you do, Death is coming for him now. And what does he do? The idiot runs." Life had been spewing this rant, with similar discussions, for the last five minutes, waving her arms wildly and strolling down the hill with long legs and intent. In her wake, the grass sprouted tall, blooming even though it wasn't the proper season. As I passed over the places where she walked, the blooms receded and the grass shortened, returning to normal. An endless cycle.

I tried to turn my attention back to the instructions, but Life finally rounded on me and jabbed me in the chest. "This is all your fault!"

I sighed and finally felt frustration rising to the surface. In true unpredictable fashion, it boiled over into uncontrollable annoyance. I batted Life's hand away, the force of the blow sending pain pulsing through my wrist. Life's eyebrows winged up and she stared at me.

"It's not my fault," I said firmly. "You were the one who called me to collect the soul of your champion. You were the one who decided that you were tired of having him around. Why would you offer such a deal to him, anyways? Are you really that stupid?"

Life took a step back and lifted her chin. "Stupid? You think I'm stupid?" She folded her arms and whirled so that her back was to me. If she was expecting an apology, she wasn't going to get one. She was just being a petulant child at this point.

"I just want to know *why*," I snapped, clenching my hands into fists, the instructions sheet crumpling in my fingers.

"Why? I'll tell you why," Life snorted. She turned to face me again, her hair whipping over her shoulder like some melodramatic television star. "Unlike my *husband*, my champions truly appreciate me. Samuel was one of the best. He appreciated every moment, living to the fullest and doing his best to eke out a living when things were at their very worst. He *loved* me, unconditionally. And I wanted that. Forever. But after I offered him the deal, everything changed. He stopped loving me unconditionally and instead used me. For pleasure. For profit. To be used like that? How dull! How disrespectful! I'd had enough, so I figured Death would help me. He *always* gets everything anyways, so why not let him, this time?"

I sighed; Life's argument actually made sense, if you took into account that she was an extremely powerful being who didn't experience things or understand the world in the same way that everyone else did. Even from a human perspective, I recognised the normality of her argument. No one likes to be used, especially when love was in its place first.

"Fine." I shook my head and unclenched my fists, the surge of emotion draining out of me and leaving me feeling empty, almost hollow. That sensation faded a moment later. "Thank you for explaining," I said, my voice back to the flat, logical tone. Life looked almost hurt by the change. "As it is, Samuel is now marked for Death, so I must go and collect his soul, regardless of what reason you had to call me in. However, I must still determine how to remove a person's soul from their body, so if you would please wait a minute, I shall finish this section of the instructions and we can go from there."

"How do you intend to find Samuel?" Life demanded, straightening her shoulders and sniffing pointedly.

"Plan later, instructions now," I said. Then, ignoring her glare completely, I stepped off the path and settled on a rock next to a scraggly, wind-stunted tree. It was uncomfortable, but did not require the coordination of moving my legs and my thoughts simultaneously.

I read.

IN MANY IMMORTAL or magical beings, their essence, the integral part of them that makes them who they are, is quite a bit different from the soul of humans. To separate the essence of these beings, you must distinguish it from their lifeforce. This should be relatively simple as they will already be marked for death and their lifeforce will no longer be the forefront energy signature. Once you distinguish the essence, then simply invoke the power that I have transferred to you and call the essence outwards, demanding that it comply to the instinct that draws it to death, to my power.

The process is very similar with humans, though the soul is a stronger energy than a lifeforce at all times. You will not need to separate the two energies, as without a soul the lifeforce will simply fade away. Again, invoke the summons and the soul should separate from the human and be collected by the orb.

Practically speaking, since you are not currently in a place where instinct serves you well, you must lay one hand on the temple of the dying and hold the orb in the other. This should initiate the separation and the orb will take care of the rest.

I LOOKED up from my reading, having gathered all the relevant information. There were still a couple of pages of instruction, but they were likely similar to the first few pages, which dealt mostly with Death's office organisation, the accounts to draw on should anything need purchasing, something about emergency contact information—oddly enough, Life was *not* on his people to call list—and a discussion of some sort of festival taking place near the edge of his lands which might need monitoring in case it spilled over.

"Very well, Life, I have a grasp of what must be done to capture Samuel's soul," I said, folding the now thoroughly wrinkled instructions away into my pocket. "I simply have to touch him—"

"Great," Life snapped, already striding on down the hill towards the nearest town. "Now we just have to *find* him."

I hurried after Life, stumbling several times over rocks and debris that she didn't even seem to notice. Some of the weeds that sprang up in her wake tangled over my shoes as they withered under my steps. I frowned and flicked the dead plants away, grimacing at the scratches their thorns made on my shoes—my Italian leather shoes.

"Seriously?!" I added a few choice words for good measure and stomped up to Life, who was already starting to roll her eyes. "Look at this! Could you maybe tone it down a bit? Your weeds scratched up my shoes! These were handcrafted in Italy, by an artisan whose family had been making shoes for two centuries and—"

"Oh, wow." Life didn't even try to hide her sarcasm. "Your poor shoes."

"Yes, my poor shoes!" I waved my hands about to the path of growth and destruction that fell in our wake. "This isn't normal, you know. You and Death, the both of you, everything just… just *does* what it's told around you, doesn't it? You just skip about on your merry business and don't even think about conse-quences, like *my poor shoes*."

Life made a sound in her throat that clearly spoke of her exasperation. She continued walking down the hill, ignoring my rant, but I was well and truly into the thick of my indignant fury, now, and kept on despite my lack of willing audience.

"I mean, think about it. Look at all the absolutely *ridiculous* situations that I've got into while working for Death: investigating a murder that he didn't commit because Justice was desperately in love with you; being pulled back to the middle of the Renaissance for good-ness' sake, just because you and Death couldn't figure out how to be in the same room for more than five minutes at a time; oh, and let's not forget the whole having to tote around *Al Capone* while dealing with a Chicago mobster fetch who couldn't get his wife to even talk with him—" I broke off, frowning. "Though, to be fair, that last one was more Death's fault than yours, but still."

"Are you getting to a point or am I going to have to listen to this all the way into the village?" Life waved her hand at the collection of stone houses that were drawing nearer. They were classic English houses, some made of the massive stone blocks common in pre-20th century houses, as well as a mix of the cement and stucco style construction of modern houses. I was distracted by them for a moment, noting the pleasant-ness of their gardens, despite the chill in the air. My indignation was too strong to ignore, though, and I quickly fell back into the rant.

"My *point* is that you and Death—you more than Death simply because of your nature, but the both of you—you just trample people underfoot without once thinking of the consequences. You act like the whole universe was created to fall at your feet. Yes, the two of you are super powerful, blah blah blah, but you don't *think*. You just do whatever you want on a whim and I'm frankly tired of it. I mean, have you ever consid-ered why it was that Samuel was so interested in taking your deal? Why he ran away from me? You just discarded him like yesterday's garbage and you're annoyed because he had the audacity to take your deal and then fall out of love with you. Get over yourself and start thinking about others for a moment!"

The last time I had felt emotion this strongly, I had discussed the relative merits of coffee and tea for nearly an hour while Agravane tried to appropriate the kettle from me. The aurai had been, over the last few days, trying to teach me how to defend myself against, well, the world. His reasoning was that just because I couldn't die didn't mean that I should throw myself into dangerous situations without care. I could still be maimed and seriously injured. Anyways, despite Agravane's training, I didn't manage to stop him for more than five seconds when he'd had enough of my tea-coffee debate.

This time, Life just shook her head, the movement making her hair sway with the breeze and sending a very pleasant scent up my nose. I sneezed.

"Have you ever considered, Cal, that all of these things are brought to you because you are so good at fixing them?"

Life didn't wait for an answer; she just lifted her chin and sauntered into the village. I paused for a heartbeat, the logical implications of that statement breaking through my emotion and restoring the height of my reason. I had to concede that the argument did have rational merit. It might not be completely accurate, and I certainly did not have enough data to determine the result, but it had potential.

I followed after Life, the scratches on my shoes nearly forgotten.

The village was fairly quiet even though the weather was decent enough that people would normally be out walking. I saw a few passers by out with a dog, coming home from the shops. Each person we passed hardly seemed to notice us all, if they did pay us any attention. Life didn't seem bothered by this, but every time I had been in the mortal realms previously, or even in Elsewhere, people at least noticed me before ignoring me. This must have been some sort of side effect to taking on Death's powers, even temporarily and incompletely.

What was even more unusual was the fact that I kept seeing glowing nimbuses, a yellow out of the corner of my eye. Each person had some colour, the strength of the colour perhaps determining how long it was they had to live. A few I saw without anything besides a tiny hint to their skin, others had a fairly consistent faint yellow halo around them. As life and I passed a shop, an old woman stepped out with a yellow strong enough to call my instincts for whatever they were to light. I stepped away from Life's side, moving towards the old woman.

"We don't have time for that, Cal," Life snapped. There was a hint of something in her voice that told me she wasn't stopping me because we had to find Samuel, but for some other more base need. Whatever it was, it was insignificant compared to what called me to do my duty.

I stepped up to the old woman and she finally seemed to see me. Her face, painted with makeup to disguise the age spots in the wrinkles, paled. Her blue eyes widened and she reached up to clasp the necklace at her throat, a cross or a crucifix. The bag in her other hand, containing freshly purchased food, fell to the ground. No one else seemed to see.

"I still have things to do," she said, her voice high and wavering.

"Leave her alone, Cal," Life repeated, stepping up to stand at my shoulder.

"I am called to this," I said. "This is what I am meant to do. I know it is your instinct to argue with me, but you and I both know that it is pointless. In this, my duty wins out over yours."

Life snorted and folded her arms, turning away from me. The woman looked between us, to entities perhaps beyond her understanding, then fell to her knees and held out her hands, supplicating. "Please, please don't take me now. I'm not ready. My son still needs me. I don't want to go. What if… am I going to hell?"

I tilted my head and pushed my glasses up my nose. "Why would you ask me that? I have no knowledge of what goes beyond. I simply release you."

To my surprise, the woman paled further, her breath starting to come in desperate pants. "You come to steal my soul and you cannot even reassure me as to where it will go? Please, please, don't do this."

I took a step forward, my left hand reaching into my pocket for the orb, my right stretching out for the woman's head. "I cannot tell you what comes beyond. That is not my role in things. Nor can I simply do as you ask. Your time has come."

The woman started sobbing, her hysterics still unnoticed by all around her. This was not a logical response, but I was also aware that most beings were not logical creatures. Still, this woman's reaction seemed a little extreme. Death is not something to fear. It simply was. I touched the woman's head before she could fall onto her face and start hyperventilating, tears streaming down. Just as I did, Life step forward and spoke.

"It was a good life," she said. One more tear

streamed down the woman's face, and then the power that I held took over.

If gaining access to Death's power was like suddenly becoming the centre of the universe, the inevitable and which all things were drawn, then exercising that power was like resignation and inevitability. I didn't know what I expected, but there was simply a sigh, a pressure against my mind and then the woman's soul was released, streaming into the orb through my body, some of its energy mingling with me, my power surging and ebbing as the soul entered then left, settling finally in the orb like a swirling mist. In that moment, I felt her fear, her pain, the anxiety that she had over a son who refused to work and who had lived off of her pension for too many years, the joy she had felt at losing a husband and the guilt that she had felt that joy. I felt everything that she felt, that she had known, and it was exquisite.

And then it was gone.

My hands trembled as I pulled it away from what was now merely a body. There was an emptiness that remained after all of that true, deep emotion. I reached up to adjust my glasses and found that my cheeks were wet. I slipped the orb into my pocket and then turned away, not wanting to see what it was that I had wrought, the reality of what was left behind after death. It was empty, used up vessel, a piece of discarded trash. And it was a human.

My soulless state of mind rebelled, pushing away that disgust after my heart tightened in my chest, making it hard to breathe. The cool, calm logic that was my norm these days returned, and I once more felt nothing, though the memory remained.

Finally, other people started to notice what had happened, a clerk rushing out from the store and screaming when she saw the woman's body. A man across the street ran over, phone already out and dialling for an ambulance. They pushed right through me, seeming to scatter the energy that I had gathered before it coalesced once more into my physical form. I staggered back, running straight into Life, who put her hands on my arms to steady me.

"It was inevitable, Cal. Much as I argue, I know as well as you do that it was unavoidable. And yet every time this happens, I feel a piece of me dislodging, floating away as though it never existed. Now do you understand why it was that Death chose you for this job?"

I pushed Life's hands away, stepping back and straightening my suit coat. I watched the kerfuffle of people swarming around the woman's body, the whine of the sirens in the distance. "No. I do not. But it must be done, so I shall do it anyways. Now, let's go find somewhere to figure out how to find Samuel Phipps."

With a move almost as unfeeling as I was at the moment, Life sniffed and turned away from the dead woman and all of those moving about, desperate to help, to return her to life. She ignored them as though they were beneath her attention, not worthy of even a moment's notice. Cruel, unfeeling, Life. She threaded her arm through mine and pointed to a coffee shop across the way.

"Come along. I will show you how to make a glamour, a guise, so that you may interact with the world and get something to eat."

"Yes, I am rather interested in what sort of coffee they have. Do you think it will be dry roasted? Perhaps a Kenyan blend? I have found that those tend to be quite good. Though I am aware that the South American coffee blends are also very popular."

Life patted my hand on her arm, the act patronising, though I did not feel offended. "Maybe we should find a sandwich shop instead."

As desperately as I longed for coffee, as I longed for the caffeine to boost my energy, to invade my system, for the taste to burst in my mouth, I had to concede that logically she had a point. If I started on coffee now, then we'd never get anything done. And I imagine that there were rather a few more souls for me to collect.

"You know Samuel's preferences, his habits and activities," I said. I pushed the remains of my club sandwich away, wrinkling my nose at the aftertaste. It wasn't quite an emotion, but it was more than nothing and so was disrupting my logical thought. I took a sip of water, washing away the taste and my thought processes went back to normal. I started again. "What I mean to say is that you are more aware of his desires and habits than anyone else. You will have a better idea of where he might go in trying to… escape? Is that his goal?"

Life shrugged and rolled her eyes. She, too, seemed a little displeased by the sandwich, but at the moment I imagined she was a little displeased with everything. If she weren't, she wouldn't have tripped the waitress with a wave of her hand in some magic, causing the woman to spill a full glass of soda onto a customer. Nor would she have blown a kiss in the direction of the chef, causing him to burn his hand on the griddle where he was reheating a bowl of soup. Life shoved her plate across the table, the scraping sound drawing the attention of many people around us, something which her guise also seemed to do. Life wasn't one for subtlety; she wore the shape of a curvaceous dark woman, her eyes a startling shade of amber. She smirked at me, as if taking note of my disapproving thoughts.

"How am I supposed to know where he would go? I didn't follow him around. I don't particularly care to know what it was that he got up to. I do know that he is not trying to escape, per se. He knows as well as anybody that you cannot escape Death—or even his temporary proxy. But you can evade it. Delay it. Subvert it." Life widened her smirk into a smile and I got the distinct impression that she was mocking me, or perhaps mocking Death. Being mocked was neither here nor there. My purpose in that moment was to determine where Samuel Phipps might end up so that I might put an end to all of this. After all, I had rather a huge amount of work to do, collecting all of the essences and souls of beings that stretched across the mortal realms and Elsewhere. Walking or flying or taking a train to each individual would be impossible, and a waste of time. I needed to figure out how to collect the souls faster, unless Death didn't expect that of me.

In short, once I got this Phipps situation under control, I could go back to the office and do some research. Read the instructions through again and perhaps discuss some of the more philosophical points with Yolanda or Agravane. Or Mercy, since the assassin was somewhat closer in understanding to Death.

"You are the one who asked for my help, so if you wish to subvert me or delay me, then I would ask you to deal with the situation on your own." I folded my napkin neatly and set it on my empty plate. As I had previously learned, the ability to feel nothing was a very useful thing when presenting a poker face.

Life rolled her eyes again, letting out a contemptuous sigh. "Fine. As far as I know, Phipps is fully aware that he can't escape you. Therefore, he shall try to eke out as much enjoyment and fulfilment from the remainder of his life as he can. I still don't have the answers you want. I cannot tell you what he enjoyed or where he spent his time. I did not care that much."

"You presented this man with a deal to extend his life indefinitely, and you did not care where he spent his time? How he utilised the life that you gave him? I thought you were upset with him simply because he did not appreciate you as he had done. That would imply a knowledge of his activities. His whereabouts." I raised my brows, waiting for an explanation. Even if I weren't in my current hyper-logical state, I would have to acknowledge the fact that Life was not a terribly rational being. She seemed to move about on whim and fancy, dealing out favours and punishments in equal turn. She was kind, she was cruel. She was good, and she was evil. She was chaotic and did not follow any set pattern that I could determine.

In my current state, trying to fathom her gave me a headache. Which was impressive, as I did not really feel pain, nor hunger, nor exhaustion. The headache must've been quite strong to break through the emptiness.

Life waved a dismissive hand. As she did, the car outside the sandwich shop swerved suddenly and ran into a post box. The horn blared and people cursed and screamed. Life placed a hand over her mouth, the smile that it hid not at all apologetic. "Oops."

"Focus, if you please."

"Fine. Killjoy. The reason I don't know about Phipps's habits or his preferences or any of that—the reason I don't know any of this about any of my champions—is because I do not care. I don't care how they spend their time, only that they appreciate me. That they love me or they hate me, that they struggle against me, determined to beat me, to get the better of me, to make the most of me. I don't care how, just that it is. Samuel—" life's eyes grew misty, the amber shade shifting into something a little more violet. "He was exceptional. He could rail against me one moment, fighting against every circumstance that I threw his way, and he could woo me the next, declaring me good and gracious and wonderful. He was my favourite... until he stopped appreciating me."

I sighed and rose, buttoning my jacket. Life frowned at me, showing her confusion. "Yes, yes, I know, you were loved and then used. As you do not seem to know anything, then I suggest a different strategy. If Samuel is meant to eke out as much life out of what he has left, that we must go somewhere where a person can experience as much life as possible."

"He could be anywhere in the world. What you suggest we do? Book a private plane and fly around until we find him?" Life stood also, sashaying past me and gathering the attention of everyone she walked by. Some people showed desire, others jealousy, others despair. I ignored all of their reactions, stepping out of the sandwich shop and thereby dropping my borrowed guise as the full effect of Death's powers came flooding back into me. Life had shown me how to put them aside for the duration of the meal, but having it back was like fitting a missing piece of the puzzle into the emptiness that resided within me.

"You can sense the strongest concentrations of people experiencing life. You may not be able to sense individuals, but you can sense the intent, the emotion, whatever it is that you call it. Simply transport us there. Then, we shall make inquiries and do it my way." I held up my hand for Life to take, the action mitigated when someone walked nearly through me, being unable to see or interact with me. I pulled my hand back so wouldn't accidentally touch the person and cause some irreparable harm. Then, I held it out again. Life simply studied it for a moment.

"It does have merit as a plan. I suppose you're not quite as useless as I thought." Before I could come up with an appropriate response, perhaps along the line of the fact that Life was the one who came to *me* for assistance, she grabbed my hand and we slipped out of existence.

Unlike before, this time it felt as though the world were rushing through us and by us. I saw flashes of the

West End in London, the beautiful cities of Monte Carlo and Macau, the flashing lights of New York City and Chicago. I will admit to flinching at the last one; my recent experiences had not left me with a particular fondness for that city. We passed through places like Everest, where people were preparing for the climb. Hollywood and Los Angeles searched around us, a hustling metropolis. We passed through mountains and forests, places with many people and with none. I saw Hong Kong and Beijing, Delhi and Paris. Next to me, Life had her eyes closed, her expression more intent than I had ever seen it.

She took a deep breath, focusing her powers so that they surged and squeezed around us, making it uncomfortable to breathe, though it would not harm me in the long run. Then, she opened her eyes, and the world solidified around us once more, taking shape in an entirely different place, one full of flashing lights and flowing water, noises and people. It was a place I had never been during my time as a normal human, but I knew of it. I would imagine they were very few people who didn't know of it.

"This is a perfectly logical place to find Samuel I would think," I said. Life took in a deep breath, obviously feeling the intense surge of purpose that came with being in a town dedicated almost entirely to living to the fullest, no matter the consequences.

"Las Vegas is not meant to be a logical place, Cal. For once, throw off that ridiculous pall that working for my husband has placed on you and just try to enjoy yourself." Life wrapped an arm around my shoulder and squeezed, even that simple act enough to send the surge of her power through me. It reacted with what Death had given me with volatility, sparking and swirling around each other like two wolves. I flinched and drew back, my own dark power gathering around my hands, the shadows appearing more vividly than I had seen them since entering the mortal realm.

"I would remind you, Life, that we are here for a very particular purpose."

Life fisted one hand on the hip, cocked it, and raised her chin defiantly. Her ever-changing and always stunning appearance seemed to shift in time with the flashing lights. I closed my eyes for a moment, trying to get my bearings, and opened them again just in time to see a surging yellow halo of light surrounding a male figure. It darted into an alleyway and I followed. I didn't know if things were going to be this easy, this simple, but I would happily follow this even if it weren't Samuel. After all, I did have a duty to fill. Some strange hopeful feeling rose inside me and I became almost thrilled to back into the alley and determine who it was that had run past. I couldn't ever see the figure as we ducked behind one of the many casinos and hotels in Las Vegas. But when we reached a parking lot, darkened and half-full with older cars, the figure turned and it became very abundantly clear that this man was not Samuel.

For one, he was perhaps twenty-five. For another, he was Hispanic, no sign of a beard, decorated with tattoos. Just another normal person in Las Vegas. Only, he walked almost directly into a small gathering of people. There was a quick exchange of words, of blows, and then someone pulled out a gun and shot him in the stomach. He fell back on the ground, the yellow nimbus flaring almost white as he fell.

The other people ran. I stopped and stood over the fallen man. He stared up at me, eyes wide, hands clutching at the gunshot wound as it ended his life.

"Madre de Dios," he whispered.

"Nothing quite so important," I said. The kid reached out a hand, shaking and trembling with blood. I sat on the ground beside him rather than taking the hand, wondering if I should just proceed and continue the search for Samuel, or if I should at least try to provide some sort of comfort in the last moments. Death had said that it wouldn't help. That my job was not to have conversations, not to theorise or explain, but to simply collect the soul. And yet, my emotions were rearing up, connecting me to the part that was still fundamentally human. And I knew that I wouldn't want to die alone with no one to explain or to sit with me.

"I can't tell you what will come after. My suspicions are that it is different for every person. I myself have never actually got that far, though once I did hear voices. Then again, that could have been my imagination as I was in rather a bad situation at the time. So I cannot provide you with that comfort, but I can tell you that it won't hurt. That all of your pain will be gone. There is no need to fear me. I am not the cause of your pain, I am the release from it."

He spluttered something, the sound gurgling and

unintelligible. I leaned closer, putting my ear near his mouth. "Get... On... With... It."

I sniffed and pulled the orb out of my pocket. "There's no need to be rude. I was just trying to help."

The dying kid coughed and growled something more, but I didn't bother to decipher or even to listen. I just tapped him on the head and experienced that same magnetic rush of power that flowed through me as his soul travelled into the orb. It was like fire overtaking my veins, surging and flaring but not burning. It was a cool breeze on a hot day, the first touch of spring, the beginning of dawn. And then, once again, the moment passed leaving me feeling empty. Emptier than before, even after the old woman. This was like one more piece of me had splintered off. Minuscule and probably negligible, but noticeable all the same.

I scowled down at the mess that the dead body made, bleeding out onto the parking lot even after his soul had departed. Now there was just biology and nature to take over, the freshly dead already attracting some flies in this desert environment. I stepped back before the blood could get on my shoes.

I put the orb back in my pocket and wandered over to where Life was waiting, her foot tapping impatiently. "Are we going to have to make a stop for every single one—"

"Until I figure out a faster way, then yes. Truly, some people are just not terribly appreciative when someone is trying to help." I pulled my glasses off my nose and cleaned them, waiting for the disappointment to fall back away into nothingness. It remained, pulsing in time with the empty feeling that the soul passing through me had left.

"People fear dying all their lives. They are afraid of experiencing it, they are afraid of experiencing its aftermath. You cannot blame them for reacting badly when you tell them that it's going to be okay, that you are here to help. You cannot tell them what comes beyond, you cannot tell them what they did before was all right. You can only exist in that singular moment of separation between body and soul. And they will never appreciate it." Life stared me straight in the eye, the effect stripping away my defences until the disappointment was laid bare in the open for all to see. It was a disconcerting feeling. "My husband has dealt with this reality for millennia upon millennia. And, if I am judging his reactions correctly, it does not become easier. Just more normal."

I nodded my head. The disappointment faded away as I had known it would, leaving me once again with absolutely nothing. Not gratitude, not anger, not joy, not hunger, not thirst, not anything. All that was left was the reasoning of my mind. And I used it.

"Well, that errand aside, if your instincts are correct then we should find Samuel somewhere in the city. I am aware that you do not know what his preference for activity is, but do you have any insight? Would he prefer to gamble or to see shows, to go to strip clubs or to, I don't know, some other entertainment activity?"

Life lifted her chin, tilting her head and considering. Finally, she twined her arm through mine and her mouth split into a feral smile. "There is little that makes one feel more alive than beating someone else out. You learned how to play poker when you bartered for Al Capone's soul. What do you say we go find a high-stakes game?"

I followed along with Life, deciding that it was perhaps prudent I didn't point out the fact that Al Capone had let me win at poker. I might have an exceptional poker face, but that did not mean I was any good at the game. Still, if it was the logical choice, then I would play. Badly, but I would play.

THE NEXT GREAT ADVENTURE

One thing I hadn't considered about Las Vegas was there were rather a lot of places a person could hold a poker game. And, a high-stakes poker game seemed just as common as a low stakes poker game. Life and I wandered into several casinos, unnoticed by any of the people. As Life passed them, people became more interested, more excited, more likely to waste rather large amounts of money on pointless games. My presence mitigated some of that, the smiles of joy disappearing almost as soon as they came. Though, I did notice that people still seemed inclined to spend rather large amounts of money despite my supposedly helpful presence.

Maybe it had something to do with a fear of dying without having accomplished something just as much as it had to do with embracing life.

I saw several more people with the glow of impending death about them, but they were not strong enough to require my immediate attention. One man feigned a heart attack at a blackjack table, but as he had no glow at all except the faint shimmer, I decided that he was faking and it wouldn't be helpful if I were to collect his soul.

Life chuckled at my disapproving glance.

After two hours wandering around the city trying to track down every dying person, we had accomplished exactly nothing. Well, that wasn't entirely true. I had managed to collect two more souls, one from a woman who looked to be in her nineties as she won a handsome amount from the slot machines, another from a spirit or Faerie creature who had been transformed into a dog and was reaching the end of its natural lifespan. The being had almost thanked me before realising what was going on, its essence swirling through me like power, but not quite as tantalising as a human soul.

"We are getting nowhere. Are you sure that he would be at a poker game?" I asked, staring at one of the many fountains that seemed to be on display outside of the hotels and casinos.

"As I said before, Cal, I cannot tell you precisely where Samuel is. I can only tell you that, for people who are trying desperately to experience as much life as they can in one short instance, beating out someone else for something desirable is a common need. Winning over a lover, getting a huge amount of money, they are both such invigorating options. If Samuel were trying to experience as much as possible before you caught up with him, then that is what he would be doing."

A street performer moved along, trying to gather interest in a show which no one seemed to want to watch. "Okay. Fine. But this wandering around is not doing us any good. Try to, I don't know, focus. Figure out where the most intense life experience is happening right now."

Life nodded and breezed in through her nose, closing her eyes on the exhale. She turned, almost a complete circle as she sought whatever indication would tell her that people were experiencing life, fighting life, whatever. I didn't need to know the specifics, though a part of me felt it necessary to gather data so that I might understand the implications later. After a moment, she pointed. At the end of her finger was, well, nothing.

Okay, not nothing. But the lights of the strip were left far behind and as we walked towards the new target, the people started becoming fewer, more desperate, the yellow tinge that followed them becoming stronger, louder. People here in this darker, more dangerous part of town, they lived differently. They were closer to the edge between Life and Death, never truly crossing one way or another.

A few of them even followed Life and I with their eyes as we walked towards what was just another bar in a town ruled by alcohol and desire. It wasn't even a very good bar, the neon open sign flickering. The windows were cloudy, the parking lot was cracked, and the single cactus out front looked as though it hadn't seen water in about a decade.

Without hesitation, Life pushed her way inside. I

followed, taking a moment to brush some desert sand from my sleeve. What we found inside was, well, like a bad television representation of what a seedy Las Vegas bar should look like.

There were booths along the wall, the vinyl done in a faded shade of scarlet, cracked with the innards showing through. The tables were lacquered over in a thick layer, reflecting the remains of spilled drinks that had long been wiped away. Peanut shells litter the floor, a tactile sensation over a carpet which had probably seen more than one dead body. And, it smelled like a wet dog. A wet, drunk dog.

The woman at the bar wore a tank top that was far too low cut for polite society. She wiped a rag over a plastic beer mug, her vacant eyes staring straight ahead. Life and I walked right past her, heading to a door that led to a back room, the word private the only shining, clean thing in the bar. An indication that no one should enter.

We entered.

This back room was far more in line with a neat casino floor than a seedy bar. The carpet was new, and industrial grey. The walls had oak panelling, with tasteful landscapes hanging on them. In the centre of the room was a single poker table at which three people were playing. One spot, meant for a fourth player, was empty, though I sensed a faint yellow haze remaining there, as if the occupant had fled only moments before, leaving part of his being behind.

I drew on the ability that Life had shown me to develop a guise that would allow me to interact with the mortal world. It left some of my Death-given abilities behind, but there was enough to still allow me to see the relative state of the other humans in the room.

They hardly blinked at my sudden appearance and only raised their brows as I slid into the fourth chair. The first, currently acting as dealer and with a large collection of chips at his elbow, was a big man, his girth probably as wide as his height. He was completely bald, unashamedly so. He wore a purple shirt which clashed terribly with the green of the table and had three massive gold rings around his fingers. The second player was a woman, perhaps forty, who looked as though she had seen the harder side of Life and embraced her, becoming a power to be feared. She was relatively fit, her bright scarlet cocktail dress out of place in the casual back room. Her blonde hair was dyed, her darker brows showing the true colour of her hair. Her fingernails were like claws, tapping on the cards. The third and final player was of ambiguous gender. I would have said male, but for the dress. I would have said female, but for the faint line of stubble on the chin. It didn't matter, whoever they were, their eyes were just as angry and dangerous as the other two.

Not that I was terribly up on such things, but I didn't think any of these people were famous. At least, if they were, it was only to the law enforcement types. Though, considering the lack of protective goons, the quiet ease at which they held themselves despite my abrupt and impossible intrusion, I doubt it very much that law enforcement knew much about these people either.

"If you're going to intrude so rudely, you might as well introduce yourself," the woman said with a decidedly Southern American drawl. I wasn't particularly capable with accents, but I would have said Georgia or Louisiana.

"Very well," I said. I settled into the chair, unbuttoning my jacket and pulling at my sleeves so they sat neatly on my wrists. "My name is Cal Thorpe. I work for Death."

Normally, the creatures who are familiar with Elsewhere or similar, react badly to that statement. They tend to get defensive or they look at me incredulously as if someone so ordinary could never be involved with someone so powerful. Humans tend to look terrified, not sure if I'm threatening them. These three just nodded and shrugged as if it were a matter of course.

"If we are maintaining polite conversation, then it would be appropriate for you to introduce yourselves." Without my asking, the large man acting as dealer started putting cards before me. The woman took a breath, as though she were used to doing so with a cigarette, and let it out just as slowly.

"You were the one who sat down at our table. I'm not sure we are meant to be the polite ones in this instance. But, since you asked, I am Jacqueline Rochefort." She took in another breath, this one obviously designed to draw attention to her chest, which I did not find nearly as interesting as the figure of a djinn who had ostensibly decided to have nothing to do with me. In my current emotionless state, I felt not even a glimmer of interest. Jacqueline seemed to notice this and quirked a brow at it. "I work for myself."

The large, gold ringed dealer spoke next. "We all work for ourselves, ostensibly." His voice was deep and gravelly, slow and deliberate. His accent was generic American, with nothing significant about it. "You may call me George."

"I am Max," the third person said, their voice as ambiguous as the rest of them. They did not even offer a hint as to their character, their occupation, nothing.

I had a feeling I was amongst the extraordinarily powerful.

"So Cal," Jacqueline said, leaning back in her chair and looking at her cards. She flipped them back to the table, her attention turning once more to me while the others examined their own hands. I looked at mine and was, well, uncaring as to whether they would allow me to win. I did not know what the stakes were, but they were irrelevant either way. I needed only information from them. A hint as to where Samuel Phipps had gone. Even gathering data as to who these people were and why they exuded such power despite being perfectly human, was unimportant.

Of course, getting the information about Samuel Phipps was not as simple as it could have been.

"So, Cal..." Jacqueline said again, tapping her fingers on the table as she appraised my facial expression, or lack thereof. "What has someone like you coming to sit at the table of people like us?"

"I believe your question as to whether or not I am interested in you as the people you are to be... erroneous. I am not. I would have sat at this table were it populated by mobsters or policemen. Of which, might I note, you are neither. I have met both and you do not fit the archetype." I placed my chips on the table, matching George's bet. Max hid the flicker of a smile beneath the drink they sipped..

"Perhaps we are and the archetype simply does not apply. Or perhaps we are not. Your powers of observation are quite acute." Jacqueline raised the bet, flicking the chips into the centre of the table with casual disregard. George shifted in his chair, the furniture creaking under his bulk.

"I'm not sure we should be giving you any clues as to who we are or what it is that we do," he said. He turned another card over on the centre of the table. No one seemed interested in it, instead all watching me for my response. Did they want me to guess what it was that they did, that they were hiding?

"I do not care what it is you do, whether you are beings of Elsewhere or of here. I do not care what sort of illegal activities you have got yourself involved in, nor whether they are perfectly legal. I work for Death. It does not matter to me what you do in life. Perhaps under different circumstances it would, but right now I am simply after a soul." And it was true, everything that I said. Granted, if I hadn't been full to the brim with Death's powers, I perhaps would have cared a bit more about their moral makeup. Then again, I was currently soulless myself, so whether they were moral, immoral, good people or criminals, it did not matter to me. Only unless it got in my way.

"Well... how interesting." Max threw the cards down, folding. "If you are not here about us, then why are you here? Why this poker game? If you truly do not care, then surely there are hundreds of thousands of other places you could be, other souls to collect. Oh... unless it is one of us that is dying?"

"No. Not yet. I am here regarding a person called Samuel Phipps. The person who was sitting in this chair prior to my arrival." I turned my cards over, showing my King and Ace and gathering more chips to sit in front of the spot where I sat. At my request, Life started prowling around the room, pausing beside each of the other players, drawing in their scent, taking in their being, doing whatever it was that she did when she took the measure of a person.

Her eyes sparked, the flash of pleasure that crossed her face a moment later signalling something perhaps disturbing. We did not have time to play her games. I was after Phipps, not another champion or whatever it was that she saw in these people.

"You may not be interested in who we are or what we do, but you should know something about us. We do not lightly give up the information of those who associate with us." Jacqueline propped her hands under her chin and fixed me with a symmetrical smile that was likely meant to be attractive. I just blinked and waited for her to finish. "What's to say that they don't turn around and rat on us?"

"The soul of the person who last sat here needs to be collected. I would not fear that they turn around and, as you say, rat on you. Phipps, if it is Phipps, will be dead. If it is not Phipps, they will still be dead. As I explained, my interest is not with the living, not with your grudges or your desires, your fears and your pains. My interest is only with your death." I refrained from looking at the next set of cards that George deposited in front of me, instead waiting for his people to provide me with the information I needed. It did not occur to me that they would not provide the information. After all, these people were obviously intelligent and perhaps opportunistic. Why else would they have let me sit at the table without putting up a fuss?

The three of them exchanged glances with one another, seeming to hold a whole conversation without saying a single word. I perhaps could have figured it out if I wished it, but I did not. I did not have any desires at that point, only the sense of duty to do what was asked of me providing motivation to continue working.

"I don't know if the person who sat there was named Samuel Phipps or something else, but he was… perhaps over-eager to play. As you entered the bar, he became agitated and left. Not by conventional means, mind you, but by a travelling spell that he had tucked away in a pocket. I believe his destination was somewhere on the East Coast, perhaps Boston." Jacqueline smiled, tilting her head and appraising my reaction. I nodded and pushed back from the table, inclining my head respectfully in gratitude for the information.

"I shall let you return to your game."

I started towards the door, life slipping into step beside me. "Oh and Cal," Jacqueline said, forcing me to turn back. "Perhaps next time our paths cross, we will both be more well-informed."

It was not a question, nor a statement that required response, so I turned and Life and I left the bar and the back room, walking back out into the sharpness of the desert night. "Well, well, I wouldn't have expected that of you Cal." Life twined her arm in mind and we started walking back towards the strip, the colourful lights acting like a sort of beacon in the dark.

"One of the reasons, I have been informed, that I was hired for this particular position by Death was that I am a capable person when it comes to dealing with other humans. For some reason, he said that people like me and it has proved useful in the past when trying to establish a marketing technique that improves a person's image and perceptio—"

Life cut me off with a hand over my mouth. I stopped talking and she dropped it, a devious smile lighting up her features. Logic told me that this was perhaps not a good thing.

"Oh I don't mean getting the information out of them. I had no doubt you could do such a thing. No I found it interesting that you could deal with them at all." The devious smile widened and Life's walk turned into a saunter. The people we passed seemed to grow taller, more confident, more full of life as we passed. Even the full strength of the powers lent to me by Death did not seem to diminish it. Curious.

"As you are likely fully aware, I am on certain as to what you are referring. These people were human. They had a knowledge of magic and of Elsewhere, but they were human. Is there a particular reason why I am meant to be wary of them?"

Life tossed her head back and laughed, the sound making a few cars swerve in the street, people laughing loudly on the sidewalk, even the light seemed to brighten. She took a deep breath and patted my arm, completely calm a moment later. "Sometimes I forget just how little you are aware of the true reality in which we live. I know that Death plucked you off of the street with little more than an introduction and a handshake, but I would have guessed that you would learn more about the world—the true world—during your brief tenure in Elsewhere. Don't give me that look, Cal. Or whatever look you would give me if you were capable of feeling frustration. If I have to spell it out for you, then I will. Those people were perfectly human, yes, but they were… more aware. Possessed of more life than the average being. Some call them clairvoyants. Others call them psychics. But unlike the adorable frauds that walk around pretending to see spirits and read palms, these people feel life. They feel the truth of things. They know something of the future. If they wanted, they could inform someone that the disaster is going to strike and become incredibly wealthy. They could provide an indication of when the stock market would climb, when opportunity would appear, when… well just about anything would happen. They are true psychics or clairvoyants. They see what people are and what people do."

That seemed reasonable enough. That explained the sense of power that I felt from those people. Not just the physical power, but the metaphorical as well. If they truly had the ability to see the future, then they would be always certain of where to stand when the world shifted. It did not necessarily mean that I should be wary of them. It just made them interesting.

Life stopped walking, fairly gaping at me. "Do you truly not understand the significance?"

"I understand the implications. They are useful. They possess an ability that many humans would give their eyes for. But, I do not see any particular need to fear them or to admire them any more than I did before. In any case, they provided the information that I required." I disentangled myself from Life, brushing off my jacket from the incessant desert air that seemed to plough particles of dust everywhere.

Life rolled her eyes. "And there I was, supposedly impressed by your ignorance. Let me guess, you wish to go to Boston?"

I nodded, fixing my glasses back on my nose after cleaning them with a handkerchief. "If it appears to be the direction which Samuel Phipps was heading, then it is logical we go there as well. I do not know where in Boston, but I'm sure you can fixate on another area of high life activity, as it were."

Life heaved a dramatic sigh, her shoulder slumping. A moment later and she extended her hand, pouting. "You can take the fun out of just about anything, can't you?"

I took her hand and before I could respond, we were shunted off through space, disappearing in a heartbeat and reappearing in another city in the opposite side of the country in another heartbeat. I didn't know where we were, except that the building surrounding us was old and made of stone and wood. There were wooden benches all over, and I turned to see some sort of steps leading to an altar or stage. Then, something landed on my face.

I jerked, brushed the thing away, saw a spider the size of a large coin crawling up my sleeve, and felt all the emotion that life thought I was lacking surge forward, making my heart beat faster, my adrenal glands active.

In short, I screamed in terror.

VEIL OF DEATH

*L*ife collapsed back on a bench, cackling, as I threw the spider as far away from myself as I could and proceeded to brush myself off, the irrational fear that another one would be crawling on me really loud at the forefront of my mind. The terror stayed longer than it should have, considering that it had been a simple surprising event. But my heartbeat stayed loud and my adrenaline high for a good thirty seconds. Even when I managed to calm down, the echo of that emotion flung itself around my innards, leaving me trembling and nervous.

I sat, just as someone came running into the massive room—what I now realised was church—eyes wide and prepared for, well, I have no idea what, considering that he was brandishing a fork. The person, a shortish man with glasses larger than my own and very little hair, wearing a tattered old sweater and some beaten up slacks, took a desperate look around, dismissing me as a threat, if he even saw me.

A moment later, I knew he must have because he sank down next to me and said, "What in the world could have made you scream like that?"

I sniffed and tried to push away the unwanted remnants of my fear. "Spider. Large spider."

The man nodded. He did not seem to have a yellow nimbus around him, so I was unsure as to why he could see me, unless there was just something about being in a church that allowed what was invisible to be made visible. Once again, the man spoke and I realised that it was simply that he was unusual, not the church.

"So… did you need pastoral advice? Or were you just running in here to escape spiders?" He smiled at me and I caught the glimpse of a deep sense of humour. A pastor. I didn't know of what denomination, but it hardly mattered. From what I understood, the beings of Elsewhere, no matter how powerful, believed in something just as humans did. Whether it was God or multiple gods, Buddha or a simple philosophy, they all believed in something. And those that ministered to such beliefs, those that spent their lives surrounded by it and nurturing it, they had an extra sense about them.

Perhaps he could tell me where Samuel Phipps had gone.

I opened my mouth to reply, but before I could, Life intervened. She was rather good at it.

"Let's go, Cal, we won't find what were looking for here." Life was suddenly standing directly before me, tugging at my hand. She looked distinctly uncomfortable, and this pastor could obviously see it. I felt my frustration rising, but it was cut off a moment later when the man spoke.

"Well, it certainly has been rather a long time since I've seen one like you. Actually, both of you seem to have something extra. Are you here because of your abilities or because something else drew you here?" He folded his hands calmly on his knees and leaned back, obviously prepared to wait for a response. Life shifted her weight, her grip tightening on my wrist.

I pulled away from Life, a thought occurring to me and taking hold in my mind. It was a thought coupled with some sort of emotion, frustration or surprise or curiosity; I couldn't quite tell which. Either way, it demanded attention and I couldn't focus on even asking about Samuel Phipps until I had dealt with it. "It seems that rather a large portion of the human world knows about Elsewhere and all that goes with it. Why are the rest of us—I include myself up until the point where I was hired by Death—So out of the loop?"

Silence descended. Life put a hand to her forehead and closed her eyes. The priest or pastor or whatever simply smiled.

"It's a matter of perception. Some people are more attuned, while others see things as people want them to be seen. But I get the impression that is not why you are here. Either of you. There is power in both of you, stronger than I have felt for a long time. You did not come for spiritual guidance, nor did you come asking questions about the state of your souls—"

"The state of my soul being that it is missing," I said,

my flat, monotone voice returned with the loss of my curiosity.

This time, I seem to have managed to startle the man, because he stared at me for a good five seconds before taking a deep breath and looking at Life, brows furrowed. She nodded, waved her hand dismissively, and looked pointedly at me.

"Cal, we don't have time for this. We have to find Phipps." Her voice had taken on a sharp edge, the intent of which jolted me into further awareness of my thus far neglected duty to collect Phipps's soul, though the sharpness did not sway me one way or another.

"Yes, this is true." I turned on the bench to better face the pastor. He held up his hand.

"I will answer your question about this Phipps person, presuming that is what you came to ask, but under the agreement we also discussed how your soul can be missing." He raised his brows, the size of his glasses barely allowing them to show over the rims. I nodded in agreement.

Life let out a snarl of frustration and strode a few paces away, sinking into one of the pews and folding her arms pointedly. "Your friend doesn't particularly like being here, does she?" It was spoken as a question but was most certainly not. It did not follow that Life would be so uncomfortable here. She was not banned by religious edict. She was neither opposed to religion, as far as I could tell. Something else must have been making her uncomfortable.

"She... does not appear to be comfortable, no," I said, having no explanation to provide.

The priest nodded. He spoke while studying her, both of us fully aware that our words could easily be picked up by her in this large, echoey room. Neither one of us seemed to care. "I have seen many who find discomfort in a church. Some for the dislike of what it represents, most for the fact that it makes them reflect on what they have done with their lives. It is not always an easy thing. Especially for one whose nature is so volatile."

I nodded, tugging my sleeves into proper position and clasping my hand around my knee which I folded over one leg. "Volatile is a perfectly accurate description. She is Life, therefore inherently volatile."

"I would be wary of referring to someone else as your life," he said with a concerned frown, at once both worried and comforting. An unusual combination. I waved off his concern.

"You misunderstand. She *is* Life. She is… the essence of life, everything that is Life. The opposite of Death. It is not a description of my relationship to her, which is perhaps more antagonistic than otherwise, but a truth. She is Life." I stopped at that, hoping that this man would understand precisely what it was that I was trying to explain, without me having to go into the metaphysics of Life and Death and Time and, well, I presume Space. It turns out that trying to have these conversations with people becomes rather complicated and occasionally delves into the realm of theoretical physics, which is particularly unhelpful when I don't understand theoretical physics.

"I see." The man frowned, looking between life and

myself. "If she is Life, then that would make you... Death?"

"Ah. No. I am simply acting as Death's proxy while he is on holiday. I work for him." This explanation seemed to confuse my conversational partner more than my explanation of who Life was. So, I was quite certain that the statements I had used were far less ambiguous when discussing my position.

"You work for Death? Do you not find that, how do I put this, morally complicated?" He gave a shrug of his hands, obviously trying to contain his dislike. He was like many mortals, and even immortals, who feared Death simply because of dying. They did not understand. Describing Life was perhaps metaphysical, but describing Death was more in the realm of poetry. And, while I was an exceptional marketing agent, poetry was slightly outside my realm of expertise.

"Death does not kill people. He simply releases them. Nor is he responsible for what lies beyond. I don't even know that, and if he did know that I very much doubt he would tell me. In any case, I am simply his marketing agent. My current position as his proxy is rather more unusual. And it is why I am here. I am searching for a man named Samuel Phipps, old, with beard, been around for several hundred years. I am meant to be collecting his soul. You wouldn't have happened to see him, would you?" I tilted my head and waited for a response, slightly alarmed to note that this man appeared to be growing all the more pale. Surely I hadn't said anything to offend him. There was nothing remotely religious or not religious in my statement, simply what I was doing and why I was there.

"Even if he had been here, which I fear he hasn't, then I am not sure I would tell you. I cannot condone such actions as yours. Collecting souls is for God, not man." He stood, brushing off his battered slacks and fixing me with a pointed stare, one that was neither threatening nor encouraging. Merely pointed. "I think it is perhaps better that you leave."

"Once again, you misunderstand. I'm simply collecting the soul because I do not have the capacity to release them on to wherever it is that they are meant to go." My explanation was too late. He was no longer listening. He strode away, walking past Life and leaving the two of us alone in a large room. Life rose from her seat, putting on all of her graceful airs, her chin lifted slightly as she came to stop before me.

"Now do you see? I do not have a problem with belief as a whole, but people so often misunderstand. They mistake intent for truth, reaction for belief, fact for falsehood. It does not matter whether or not what they believe is true, only that they are blind to everything else. Not all are like this, but many." Life held out a hand to assist me to my feet. As I did not require assistance, I ignored it and rose, though I will admit I did glance after the pastor in confusion.

"I could have explained that neither you nor Death was contradictory to any of his beliefs, but he did not appear to wish to listen." Never once had the man even asked me what I thought about all of this, what my position was on belief and faith. It was irrelevant, but it was curious. I turned to Life. "Why was it, may I ask, that your focus brought us here? I would not think that a place such as this would be the first place you would go."

Life took in a deep breath, eyes wandering over the eaves and the carved wood, the sconces and the windows. She shook her head. "For all that humans are a blind species, even those who see more than we expect, when they devote their life to something, they do it wholeheartedly. The people who come here apparently have devoted their whole life to it."

I nodded, because it seemed like the only appropriate answer that I could give. Truth be told, even with all the logic at my disposal, I did not entirely understand. Then, there were many things, in both the mortal realms and Elsewhere that I still did not fully grasp. I assumed that further understanding would come with experience and thus, the passage of time. Though, I had met Time and he did not seem to have a full grasp of things either.

Then again, I was fairly certain that Time was slightly insane.

I followed Life out of the church and onto the bustling streets of Boston. It seemed stark compared to the ridiculous extravagance of Las Vegas, but there was more purpose here, more intent. There were far more people walking around with yellow signatures of varying sorts of following swiftly on behind. None of them required my particular attention, as they were not strong enough to indicate that someone was dying, but then Life and I turned a corner and a series of massive buildings rose up before us, almost their entire architecture glowing golden.

I had to go in. There were souls in there waiting for me to collect them. Samuel Phipps would have to wait.

As soon as I approached the glowing building, I realised that it had been a mistake. Okay, not an actual mistake—there were most definitely souls here that I needed to collect—but more of an unfortunate set of circumstances that may not have set off an emotional storm, but certainly could have done.

It was a hospital.

I hate hospitals.

My dislike for the places had been present back in my life as a normal human in the mortal realms, thanks to an unfortunate incident with a motorised scooter. The scooter had won and I spent several months in and out of a hospital to deal with the two broken bones and a lingering concussion. I had been ten.

Then, after shaking hands with Death to seal our employment agreement, the effect of his power on me had been so strong that I blacked out and ended up in a hospital with Doc Graveltoes staring down at me. The Doc is some sort of tiny gremlin goblin thing and has absolutely enormous, bulbous eyes. Waking to find the thing staring down at you was more than a little terrifying. Such had been my introduction to the world of Elsewhere.

I stepped farther into the entrance of the building, feeling an uncomfortable sort of strain in my stomach. It wasn't emotion, per se, but it was enough to make me frown, even in my current state. Life sighed dramatically and propped a hand on her hip.

"You can't be serious," she grumbled. "You have to stop *here*?"

"It's not like I really have a choice," I retorted. I started towards the strongest glow, assuming that would be where the dying people were. "My duty to Death requires that I collect the souls of all those whose life has come to an end. I cannot simply swan off to follow *one* soul at the expense of all the others. As it is, I've probably wasted too much time chasing after Phipps. I have souls all over the mortal realms—and Elsewhere—to collect and we have been going too slowly. So, yes, we're stopping."

Life rolled her eyes but followed me. We slipped past various medical staff, some in scrubs, others in white coats. It all seemed fairly calm, if a touch frenetic. Not at all like those ridiculous medical dramas that Yolanda and Agravane made me watch. At least they'd moved on from some of the more melodramatic soap operas after Agravane and I essentially experienced our own in Chicago.

The first floor seemed to have mostly testing facilities, and the doctors, nurses and patients I passed all had normal shades of yellow surrounding them. They might have been exhausted, but they weren't dying. Then, Life and I wandered through a set of heavy doors that had all sorts of notices and warnings on them and I knew we were in the right place.

The air here felt sharper, as though everyone held their breath as they walked through. The sounds were also both muffled and more precise; what little noise there was grated on the ears because it was in such contrast with the oppressive quiet. The lights were dimmer than the other area we'd passed through. And there was a definite surge of bright golden-yellow light from all but three of the rooms.

I stepped into the first one.

"Are you here to do more tests?"

Life sucked in a breath. The speaker was a child, a girl of no more than seven. She was tiny compared to the bed surrounding her. The blankets were perfectly smooth around her form except for the tubes that seemed to engulf the child. Her eyes were wide, too big for her too-thin frame. Her skin should have been a healthy dark tan, but was now pallid. Her dark hair was lank around her shoulders. She clutched a well-worn teddy bear to her chest.

"Cal, please," Life said, stepping forwards and reaching out to the girl. Life looked back at me, desperation plainly visible on her face. The girl eagerly lifted her hand to grab Life's. She should have burned to ash at the touch; too much Life was just as deadly as not enough. Instead, the girl remained as she was. Ill. Dying.

"You know I must," I said softly. Now would have been a great time for me to break out of that logical fugue which I bore. I knew that I shouldn't have thought that. Thinking such a thing was indicative of strong emotion just as much as a clench in my chest was emotion. But I *felt nothing,* and I knew I should. Biologically speaking, it was ingrained in me to want to protect children. The survival of the species depended on it. There was still nothing in me that felt I was connecting to the child, laying there with her eyes wide and desperate, a weak smile on her face as if Life and I were the nicest people she'd met in a long time. And the fact that I felt nothing weighed on me more than I can say.

"Cal, *no,*" Life said, her eyes brimming with tears. "Not this one. *Please.*"

"What's wrong?" the girl asked, patting Life's hand. Life shushed the girl gently and brushed her hair back from her face.

"Nothing, dear one, just go to sleep."

"I'm not tired," she said. "Not anymore."

The light around her grew stronger, strong enough that it seemed to make her very bones glow through her skin. I knew that the girl had surely already died, that there was nothing that could be done for her, that all I could do was untether her soul and collect it in the orb in my pocket. Still, I hesitated long enough to try to explain.

"My dear child," I said, stepping forwards and holding out my hand. "Do you know why I am here?"

"For more tests?" She blinked those enormous eyes.

Life glared at me as though I was more than Death's proxy, as though I was cruel.

I shook my head. "No," I said. "No more tests. You will have no more tests ever again." I extended my hand farther, waiting for her to take it, my other hand slipping into my pocket to brush up against the orb so that I wouldn't have to let her see what I was doing, how the orb glowed with other souls that I had collected. The girl hesitated.

"But I'm still sick," she pointed out.

"No," I said. "You are not sick. Not anymore."

"The doctors told my dad that I wasn't getting better," the girl said after a moment, her eyes growing old as I looked on. She was starting to understand. Beside her, Life was quietly sobbing, unable to watch the young child slip away from her. "You're here to take me away."

"Yes," I said. I extended my hand even closer, knowing that I could just touch her on the head and the deed would be done. Something in me asked that I wait for her to reach out, that I wait for her to understand.

"Are you God?" She looked a little confused, like I didn't fit with her image of what God should look like.

"No," I said. "I am merely a moment. A transition to what comes next."

The girl nodded solemnly, as if she had grasped what it was I said, even if I did not fully have the data and logic to explain it all. Life made a sound in the back of her throat, somewhere between furious and desperate. She reached out to bat my hand away, but the girl got there first, our fingers brushing only the tiniest amount.

It was enough.

As before, the power of the girl's soul flowed through me, invigorating and marvellous and like a drug that I had grown too fond of. I loved it, craved it, wanted the power and impossible potential of a soul to fill me more than just temporarily. Mentally, I grasped onto the soul as best I could, trying to hold on to it. I heard the girl's shock in my head, and then the moment was gone. The soul had slipped into the orb where it coalesced with the others, precisely where it needed to be and so far out of my reach.

I opened my eyes, not realising that I had closed them. The body of the girl lay there, flat and empty, her fingers limp against the bed. Shadows swirled around me, darker than I had seen them anywhere but around Death. They seemed to be taking in any remaining energy, whether that was from where the girl's soul had lingered or if it was residual lifeforce that she had left behind. Without my permission, my hands shook.

"You bastard," Life hissed at me. She took a step towards me, her hands clenched into fists at her sides. Her ever-changing hair swirled around her like fire, echoing her fury. "She was nothing more than a *child*! She had so much life left to live, so much she could have offered the world!"

"And yet she was dying. Is that my cruelty, or yours? I simply released her soul, as was required of me," I explained, tilting my head. "Your behaviour is irrational; I am aware that you are Life and therefore not always required to be rational, but even you must know that I was not the cause of her difficulties. Surely your husband has explained such things to you before."

Life did not dignify that with a response. She just brushed by me, her shoulder ramming into mine as she strode from the room. "I will be outside, trying to think of where Samuel could be. I won't stand around and watch you *kill* my people."

She did not seem to be understanding what I was trying to say. I wasn't killing people, just removing their souls. But Life did not appear to want to listen, nor to hold a proper discussion of facts. Life just left.

I shook my head, but acknowledged that there was no explaining facts or logic to some people. Yolanda, for example, could not seem to understand that it was scientifically proven that too much salt was bad for you. She simply ate huge amounts of salt anyways and ignored all the medical journals I placed around. Life appeared to be of the same mettle.

It did not matter. I had more souls to collect and did not have time to stand around musing on the nature of Life or logic. I stepped out of the girl's room just as a man with bags under his eyes—who I presumed to be her father—stepped in and saw the remains of his daughter. I turned down the hall, oddly aware of the sobs emanating from that room.

The next two rooms I entered were both people well into their older years, both of whom seemed to accept my touch without requirement for any explanation or commiseration. The third person whose soul I collected did not even wake when I touched his head, just silently passed on, his soul pulsing through me like life-giving water.

Each soul I collected seemed to be harder and harder to let go, though they all inevitably slipped through my grasp and into the orb. I *wanted* the soul more than I had wanted anything in my life. I tried to remember when I had wanted something more, but all I could think about was the raw power that flowed through me every time I touched someone. It was tantalising, like something I knew I needed to live but couldn't have.

It was a drug, and logic told me that my growing cravings were unhealthy, that I should distance myself emotionally from the souls, but what I felt wasn't emotion, it was *need*. So I walked through the rest of the hospital, collecting twelve more souls and nearly sobbing from desire as I reached the last room. My hands now would not stop shaking.

"Well, it's about time you got here."

I looked up, taking carefully measured breaths to try to bring my physical reactions under control. A woman in her middle years, perhaps a bit round and not entirely attractive, quirked an eyebrow at me. She took a rattling breath and her chest trembled as she did. Her hair was completely gone, covered by a ratty hat. From the way she breathed, she could barely move. And yet, she was practically glaring at me.

"You were expecting me?"

"I wasn't expecting *you*, as such," she snapped. "Just someone… you know."

"You were expecting Death," I said. She jerked her head once in confirmation. "I am acting as his proxy."

"Proxy? Why? Am I not good enough to deserve his personal attention?" She was definitely angry about something. I suspected that it had little to do with me and more to do with the fact that I was here and therefore a convenient target.

"Death is currently on holiday," I explained. "I am managing the collection of souls in his absence."

"Right. Sure." The woman snorted, which set of a round of coughing. She tried to bring a hand up to cover her mouth, but her fingers barely twitched. I could have snuck forwards and taken her soul while she was incapacitated, but something held me back. Desire and craving pushed me forwards, but something most definitely held me back. I waited in the doorway, my hands stuffed into my pockets to hide the way the shadows danced around them, aching and desperate.

The coughing fit subsided and the woman deepened her glare at me. "I've been waiting nearly a full day."

"I got here as fast as I could," I replied, stating the literal truth. This earned me a derisive snort.

"Great. Death hired an idiot to act for him in his stead," she sneered. "I'm over here dying of lung cancer and you march in here with an 'I got here as fast as I could'. We're not supposed to have to *wait* for *Death*."

"My apologies," I said, finally stepping into the room. She was not going to invite me in, so I would have to enter on my own. I approached her bed and could see the fury in her eyes. It was so much like Life's fury that I blinked, half-expecting Life to appear. The woman waited for an explanation, but I had none to give. "I have been moving as quickly as I can while collecting souls, but I only possess a small portion of Death's powers. It would seem that rapid collection is not among them."

"That's the worst answer I've ever heard," the woman snapped. She took in another rattling breath, sending the machines around her haywire. No one came to turn off the machines or to even see if she was alright. They must have heard the noises before. After a while, it became pointless to rush in every time a dying person's system did something it wasn't meant to do.

"I have no other answer to provide." I could just reach out and touch her, brush my hand over her arm and her soul would pass through me, giving me another touch of power, another taste of that potential. My right hand almost came out of the pocket before I recalled myself and was able to force it to stay put.

"Find one," the woman demanded. "You're moving too slow. You're letting people *suffer*. You're putting people through the worst thing that could ever happen to them and saying that it's fine because, what, you'll get there, eventually? Do you have any idea how many people die on Earth every single day? Are you just going to walk from soul to soul? The world will end before you can manage that. And in the mean time, we're all going to suffer more pain than you could ever imagine."

Her words struck me like a physical blow, but instead of recoiling, my emotions surged upwards. I leaned over her and sneered, feeling indignation and hurt at the insinuation. "More pain than I could ever imagine? I've had my throat slit more than once. I've been impaled on a stalagmite. I've been shot. I've been crushed by a steel girder. I've been disintegrated while standing between *Life* and *Death* as they fought. Don't think that I don't understand pain. I *know* pain."

She thrust her chin out, perhaps the only movement of defiance that she could make in her currently weakened state. "Then why would you allow us to suffer?"

I baulked. She was right. I understood what it was to feel pain, perhaps more than anyone I'd ever met. I literally couldn't die, but my pain receptors were extremely active. I knew what it was to have my spine flattened under an impossible force. I knew what it felt like to have someone rip the life from me violently, and I knew what it felt like to have injuries that wouldn't kill me but would add up until there was literally nothing else for me to do but black out from the pain. And, even in my most logical state, even when I was acting like a psychopath who had no emotions at all and didn't simply kill people due to some morals that I had accepted, I would never wish that sort of pain on anyone else. I might have been empty, soulless, but I wasn't cruel.

"I do not know how to move any faster. I do not know how to be in two places simultaneously," I explained, swallowing back my despair even as it reared up inside me and made my eyes water. I pulled my hand out of my pocket and wiped at my eyes, smudging my glasses lens in the process. "Death… my instructions did not extend that far."

"Great. Just great. Some idiot is making us suffer, and he's not even doing it on purpose. *Death* is." She wheezed out what I assumed was meant to be a laugh. Then, she fixed me in her gaze, the anger and the disgust and all the derision gone in favour of desperation. "Can't you, I don't know, concentrate or something?"

"I can try," I said. I pulled the orb out of my pocket and closed my eyes. My heart seemed to beat faster as I brought my other hand closer to the woman and concentrated. The orb seemed to grow warmer in my hand, as if I was mere moments away from tasting once again that transcendent power that each soul possessed.

My hand grew closer to the woman. I tried to hold it in check, concentrating on that yellow nimbus of energy that surged around each person as they neared death. As their souls neared escape. I could almost see the glow through my closed eyelids, the draw of it so much stronger than it had been before. Sweat beaded on the back of my neck.

I couldn't resist the pull any longer, reaching down to touch the woman on her temple, the surge of power that released her soul sending sparks through my body. The power rose within me, this time meeting the energy from the soul with a roar of its own. The woman's soul flowed through me, touching and tempting me to reach out and grab onto it. I tried to do just that, but when I did, I suddenly fractured into a thousand pieces.

I screamed, the physical discomfort of the process overcoming any emotion or lack of emotion that I felt. My eyes were forced open and the impossibility of what I saw nearly made me black out. Or perhaps that was the shadows whirling at the edge of my vision, the extension of Death's power rising to the forefront. I was in the hospital room with the woman. And I was in India in the room of an old man surrounded by family. I was in an alleyway with a homeless woman. I was in a factory in Asia somewhere. I was on a boat at sea. I was drowning. I was falling. I was being shot. I was torn apart. I was falling asleep after a long life. I was *everywhere*. And I witnessed and felt every death.

I touched each person as the moment came and called to me, the souls flowing forwards without a hint of resistance. My body sang with joy as the unfettered power of those souls, of the essence of those beings from Elsewhere who lived in the mortal realms, moved through me. Then, it became too much.

I suddenly couldn't breathe, choking on that power. My heart was beating too far. My eyes became unable to see, instead surrounded by whorls of white and shadow. My head was screaming in pain.

I fell apart, exploding into a thousand pieces. I was dying. I was dead.

And then, like every time before this, I wasn't.

From a thousand locations and deaths, I pulled back into my body at the hospital, the souls and essences of those deceased people following beside me. They coalesced into the orb and I fell to my knees, screaming in lingering pain. Every muscle was on fire and I barely managed to grab the orb and shove it into my pocket before blacking out on the floor.

My last thought was that none of the deaths I had just caused or experienced belonged to Samuel Phipps. But I knew, somehow, where he was.

DEATH IS THE UNIVERSAL CURE

I shuffled out to meet Life a few minutes later, physically sore and unable to move at full speed. Sometimes, the after effects of having, well, *died* lasted longer than otherwise. I found that full disintegration usually left me sore for a couple of days. Life took one look at me and started laughing.

"You look terrible," she grinned. I shuffled over, my knees screaming at me to stop moving, and collapsed on the bench next to her.

"Thank you," I grumbled, feeling emotionally sore as much as physically sore. I knew that it would fade away soon, but I revelled in the ability to feel grumpy about being torn to pieces when I dealt with such a massive amount of death. "It's so nice to know that my efforts to do precisely as I have been ordered and collect all the dying souls of the mortal realms leaves me looking as bad as I feel."

Life snorted and tilted her head to the sky, revelling in the early morning rays of dawn. I wanted to sock her over the head. "Relax, Cal. It's not like you can truly die, you know. It's just a little pain."

"A little pain? A *little* pain?" My voice was growing unnervingly high. I resisted, barely, reaching out and wrapping my hands around Life's throat to throttle her into submission. "Being torn apart into a thousand pieces, that's only a little *pain*? You knew this was going to happen! If I collected the souls all at once, like I was meant to, then I would be torn to pieces. Is this why Death has *me* acting as his proxy while he's on holiday?!"

"You are very melodramatic," Life said. She stretched her arms out on the back of the bench. It did not occur to me that she was perhaps revelling in my pain until much later. It made sense; I had just defied her as Death defied her. She was probably still pissed, but she needed me. The least she could do was enjoy my misery.

I huffed and folded my arms, slouching. "Do you know, it gets old. The two of you messing around with us mere mortals, playing games and leaving out crucial information? It gets really, really old."

Life turned and faced me with a cat-like smile, showing all her teeth. "And yet, you still work for Death without an argument."

"I would happily argue with him, but whenever I get the chance, he explains things in a reasonable manner. It's very annoying," I retorted, settling deeper into my slouch. Life chuckled, her smile widening. She obviously felt no sympathy for me whatsoever. "Oh, go kick an ostrich," I snapped.

Her eyes widened, and she made a very unladylike sound in the back of her throat. I think she was laughing at me. "You want me to *what*?" She clapped her hands delightedly.

"Kick. An. Ostrich," I said. "Especially considering that they kick back."

"Cal, you really are wasted on my husband. How about you work for me instead?" Life reached out to brush a hand down the side of my face. It didn't work out quite the way she planned, as both my hunched posture and my glasses got in her way, but she did give it a try. I narrowed my eyes at her.

"And do what, exactly? You don't need any more marketing than you're getting and I've seen how you treat your champions."

Life tossed her head, a breeze that wasn't there bringing the scent of her hair closer to me. If I was meant to enjoy the scent, or feel *anything* about it, then it didn't work. I scowled deeper, practically feeling the frown lines burning into my forehead. I didn't care.

"Oh, it wouldn't be anything like making you one of my champions," she said, waving a dismissive hand. "Your inability to die makes that an impossible option. There have to be consequences, after all. No, I'm thinking more like an errand runner. Someone to… do the things I need done all over Elsewhere and the mortal realms. It would be so interesting to see you interact with all those people."

I sniffed and grumbled under my breath. Life stared at me, waiting for a response and I realised that she was serious. "This is ridiculous. Why would I come work for you? You've been nothing but unhelpful and cruel to me in the entirety of our acquaintance. The only reason I'm helping you, now, is because Death needs me to collect souls and Samuel Phipps's soul needs collecting."

Life leaned in close, her whirlpools of eyes doing their best to entrance me, to draw me in. It would have worked well, except for the fact that I could already feel my grumpy mood falling away. It was still there, enough to note the draw she had on my emotions, but it was swiftly being replaced by cold, hard logic. And even logic was telling me that working for Life had too many downsides and not one upside.

"I can stabilise your condition," Life breathed in my ear.

My logic faltered.

"It's not possible," I returned, but my voice had a definite hitch to it that had nothing to do with emotion. "Death has researched a dozen different means of stabilising my condition until I can find my soul and has come up with nothing."

Life pressed her hand against mine, her fingers burning my skin. I pulled away, straightening my posture and doing my best to fix her with a disapproving glance. Given the way that she continued to smile at me, I was forced to assume that my attempt had failed.

"Cal, there is something very fundamental that you seem to be forgetting," Life said, folding her hands neatly on her lap and leaning back against the bench. "I am not Death."

That… was a relevant fact.

Life was *not* Death. She did not have the same limitations as he did. She was not bound by his rules. He, of course, was also not bound by her rules or her limitations. Their capabilities were not the same, by any means. Did that mean where Death had failed, Life could succeed?

"I will have to consider the full implications of what you suggest," I said, my voice still wavering even as monotone as it was. Life nodded and hummed, her lips pressed together but obviously still smiling. She had me. She knew she had me. All the logic in the world could not refute the simple fact that she could be telling the truth.

"Well, anyways, I'm sure you'll be wanting transportation back to Elsewhere, now?" Life asked, casually extending her hand.

"Why would I want that?" I asked. Yes, this was an important decision and I would have preferred to think about it in my office, but our task in the mortal realms was not yet done. "Samuel Phipps's soul has not yet been collected."

Life rounded on me, surging to her feet and staring down at me with wide eyes, hands clenched at her side. "*What?*" she said, voice low. "I thought you collected all the souls from the mortal realms. I *felt* them go!"

"I don't know what you felt, but I do know that Samuel Phipps was not amongst the souls I gathered. I think it might have something to do with the fact that you provided him with extra protection for such a long period of time."

"How dare you blame—"

"I know where he is," I said. Life froze with preternatural stillness. She quirked a single brow. "He is in a very small town in the mountains of India. Near Nepal. It seems a strange place to find him, given all the theories we proposed about his wanting to seek out a way to fill his life to the fullest."

"Give me your hand," Life demanded without providing an explanation. I hadn't expected one, to be fair. I reached out, my sore muscles protesting, and grabbed her hand. Boston disappeared around us, fading into nothingness. Logic aside, I cannot say I was sorry to see it go.

When the world reappeared again, my physical soreness screamed defiantly at me, then gasped and limped quietly away. I was still in pain, but it seemed secondary to the fact that I was having a difficult time getting enough oxygen into my lungs. That, and the air was cold. Really cold.

"Isn't it bracing?" Life asked, spreading her arms wide and taking in a lungful of insufficient air. "There's such extremeness, living in a place like this. It breeds strength!"

"Urglhfrlghl," I managed, coughing as I wheezed in some cold air. "A little warning would have been useful."

"You'll get over it," Life said, waving her hand in dismissal. "Now, the village should be somewhere right around here, no?"

I pointed to a collection of very low buildings made of stone and thatched with some combination of grass and mud. They looked very solid, very sturdy, and wholly improbably in an environment of vast rocks and scrub grass, where the very trees were stunted and twisted, the only sign of non-plant life that of an eagle very, very far above us. It was striking, objectively speaking, and unlike anywhere I had ever been. However, given that my finely crafted suit and now-scuffed Italian leather shoes were doing absolutely nothing to keep out the cold, I doubted that I would be returning to this place after Samuel Phipps had been found.

Life strode towards the village as if she had been living on next to no air for years. I followed after, my body feeling as though it was swimming through pudding. Eventually, I made it to the village and caught up with Life. She smirked at me and flounced onwards. Unable to do otherwise, I followed.

"There's no one here," I pointed out after a few minutes of wandering around the village. I did not point this out just to take a moment to rest, but logic told me to take advantage of a decently sized rock and sit while we discussed our options. I obeyed logic.

"Of course there are people here," Life scoffed. She waved her hand to the village which looked thoroughly abandoned. "Can't you feel their souls?"

I could, if I closed my eyes and concentrated on any future deaths. But the tantalising call of people's souls was faint, as if very far away. Either that, or I was suffering from oxygen deprivation. I opened my eyes and saw Life walking away from me, heading to the place where the concentration of souls was the strongest. I pushed myself off of the rock and followed her, gritting my teeth as I trudged uphill.

The crest of the hill was more like a tiny plateau before the whole world ascended into the mountains that towered over us. But it was enough to allow one more stone house, this one half built into the rising stone. Life paced outside, flashing her eyes at me when I arrived.

"Do you feel them, *now*?" Life hissed in my ear, staring towards the entrance of the house.

I could. There were two souls in there, near to death. Calling out for me to take them, to touch them, to pull them into my system and feel the pure *power* that they could provide. I blinked and pulled back my senses, mentally shaking myself. That was most assuredly not an emotion, and nor was it logical thought. That was... addiction?

It was similar to the pull towards coffee that I experienced every morning. While I loved coffee—it was just such a beautiful liquid, providing warmth and energy and happiness. There was such flavour and—I shook myself again. This was more than my affection and addiction for coffee. This was something far deeper.

I pushed my way into the house, ignoring the creak of the door as it opened, mindless of the packed dirt of the floor, the brightly coloured fabric that covered the windows, and turned towards the tiny room where the souls pulsed. Inside was a bed, occupied by a figure nearly covered with quilts to keep out the chill of the mountain air. I barely registered the figure as a girl before my attention was drawn to Samuel, watching me warily from the corner. He had a knife in his hand, poised to attack me if I came any closer. It wouldn't stop me from taking his soul and that of the girl who was obviously sick.

"Caught up with me, did you?" It was phrased as a question, but it wasn't. Phipps knew precisely what was coming next. It was apparent in the drawn lines around his mouth, the dark skin where his beard did not grow. I shuffled closer to the girl. "Wait. Please," he said, the sound falling from his mouth like stone.

It was enough to pull me out of the craving for the momentary feel of that power, the touch of a soul. I straightened, just realising that my shoulders had hunched and my fingers were twitching. I pulled at the sleeves on my jacket and set my shoulders square. "Why here?" I asked, my voice flat as my unemotional state reared its head again.

"Didn't she explain it to you?" Phipps asked, jerking his head to where I assumed Life stood behind me. "She knew I would be here. Isn't that how you found me?"

I turned to Life and tilted my head in question. Life rolled her eyes, fisting a hand on her hip. "I *had* hoped for something more original, more in line with your previous admiration for me. But, yes, I suppose I knew you would be here."

I turned back to Phipps, this time tilting my head at him.

"Do you know that when she 'extends' your life, effectively granting you immortality, that you can't interact with the mortal world in a normal way?" He looked desperate, the knife in his hands wavering as his hands shook.

"I am aware that immortality changes one's perspective," I said, stating fact.

Phipps frowned at me, then shook his head. He continued. "Well, I didn't understand what it really meant until it was too late. She offered me immortality. I took it. But I couldn't have any more children. I couldn't *change*. I was just… stuck."

"Interesting. You are suggesting that the particular means Life used to extend your existence prevented you from changing. Therefore, your inability to feel boredom continued and was the reason for your many centuries of extended life." I nodded; that was not a logical progression that had occurred to me.

"What? No. Seriously, weren't you listening?" Phipps frowned at me, though I was unsure as to the cause. "My bloodline is dying. I could no more help it than I could die myself. And now the last remaining member of my *family* is…" His voice cracked and tears started forming in his eyes.

"She is dying," I said, assuming that was the end of the sentence that he could not manage to say, due to emotional entanglement. Phipps glared at me, lifting the knife higher, the shaking in his hand dissipated.

"Don't you *touch* her," he growled. "She is the last of my family. The last chance I have to make things right. And she's dying. I will *not* let you take her!"

I looked at the girl for a moment, noting that her dark golden skin was looking pale, that her lips were dry and cracked and that she stared at me through rheumy eyes. She knew I was there and was, therefore, close to taking her final breath. I needed to take her soul, to release her from the suffering of her lifeforce and gather her into the orb. I reached my hand into my pocket to touch the object in question, as cold and still as ever, despite the number of souls that it carried.

"She *is* dying," I said, trying to point out the facts so that Samuel might see the truth. "Her soul calls out."

"No!" He stepped forwards and put his knife at my throat. I did not pull back, but nor did I advance. His behaviour was irrational from someone who knew first-hand the cruelties of Life. Would it not be better to release this girl, some great-great-great niece or other, from her pain?

"I do not understand," I said. "What would you have me do? I am an agent of Death. I *must* collect the souls of the dying. If I do not, then Death certainly will when he returns. All that will get you is maybe a few more days with her. A few more days where she suffers."

Phipps pressed the knife closer to my throat. The tip cut the skin open and blood dripped down, likely staining the collar of my shirt. I waited. Surely he would make his point soon.

"Do you know why she's dying?" Phipps demanded. I shrugged.

"No. I only know that she is dying. Does it truly matter?" I asked. I could feel Life pressing closer behind me, though she thankfully said nothing. She was, it seemed, simply content to watch this inevitable battle between an agent of Life and one of Death.

Though, past experience told me that she would step in as soon as she thought that things were going against her. That was simply her nature.

"She can be *cured*!" There was desperation in his voice, a sound that I had heard many people make before, when they held onto a scrap of hope that was futile. Pointless. Illogical. I looked at the girl again, noting that her breath had become more ragged. She would not last long and I needed to sever her soul now.

I opened my mouth to say as much when Life, as expected, cut in. "Samuel," she purred, "surely someone who has seen so much life knows the futility in such a thought."

Okay, that went against expectations. What was Life up to?

"She was stolen as a baby to be replaced by a changeling child. I got her back," Phipps said, pressing the knife closer to keep it from trembling in his hand. "She needs food from Faerie to bring back her humanity!"

Life clucked her tongue as if Phipps' explanation meant something to her. It meant nothing to me, despite my recent encounters with beings who were Fae—a fetch and a banshee, now in the witness protection program. I was not aware of Fae lore and did not know if such a condition was real, or if it could be reversed. I flicked my eyes towards Life, who was watching Samuel Phipps hungrily.

"Can her condition be cured, even at such a late stage?" I asked. Why had I asked? I knew that she was meant to die; the yellow glow around her being told me that. So why was I fighting against her death? Why was I suddenly considering advocating letting the child live? It went against my contract with Death and, what's more, was highly illogical. Unless...

Unless I wanted to see whether Life could actually help me.

The thought struck me silent, and I hardly heard what was said next.

"... Once there, you could theoretically make a play for some food to fix a changeling child, but it would not be easy," Life finished. I did not care what she had said before. I could not let her know that I was distracted because I was thinking about her offer. I would not give up working for Death, but I wanted to consider what Life could do for me. And it went against everything I did not feel.

"And you," I said, nodding my head at Samuel, heedless of the fact that my movements made the knife bite into my neck quite deeply. My vision flashed white for a brief moment and I returned to myself, once more dead and not dead. Samuel stared at me with wide eyes, already retreating a step, the knife and his hand covered in my blood. I touched my neck, just to be sure that I wasn't bleeding anymore. All looked healed.

I nodded again and continued. "If we do this and save your bloodline, will you go with me, giving up your soul without a fight?"

"Yes," Samuel said without a moment's hesitation. He licked his lips and said it again. "Yes, I will happily die for her sake."

I adjusted my glasses on my nose and started to

brush at the lapels of my jacket, frowning as I encountered my blood. "You do realise that I could simply call both of your souls to me this very moment? If I do this, then there must be a reason. A payment."

Samuel closed his eyes, his throat bobbing beneath his beard. He opened them again and looked between Life and myself. "You won't do this simply because she can be saved?"

"No," I said, my voice flat even for my emotionless state. At least, it felt like my emotionless state, even if I was turning my situation over and over and over again in my mind. Considering my options, that wasn't emotion, was it? I returned my focus to the matter at hand. "I work for Death, not Life. I will not save her simply because she can be saved. I require a price."

The words were not what I intended, but they were true. Death would not do something simply because it could be done. That wasn't who he was. It was who *Life* was, but not Death. He would demand a payment. No wonder people hated him, for all my marketing efforts.

"She will owe Death a favour," I said, the pronouncement like stone from my tongue. Solid, harsh, immutable. "On her sixteenth birthday, Death will come and collect his payment."

"So soon…" Samuel muttered. But there was something in his eyes as he looked at the girl that told me he would accept. "It won't be *her* death he demands?"

I considered, waiting for instinct to take over as it had moments before. "No," I said. "Not hers."

Samuel nodded once, shoved his knife into the belt on his trousers, then grabbed my hand and shook.

There was a burning sensation for a moment, a glow that was something like the yellow nimbus that surrounded him and the girl, and then it was gone. Samuel's soul was still in his body, the girl was still breathing, and my hand felt warm where the bargain stuck to my skin, surrounded by shadows. What an unusual sensation.

I looked at Life. "Alright, you got your wish. I'm fighting for you. For now. Now how do we get to… wherever we have to go?"

Life grinned, her teeth suddenly pointed like a shark. "To the Goblin Market? Simply follow me."

She turned and, as if parting a curtain, stepped through the rock wall that made up the back of the stone house. The wall shimmered in her wake, a portal to some other place, some other world, one that I did not know. Samuel did not hesitate in stepping after her, only sparing a single glance for the girl in the bed.

I took a moment longer. "What is your name?"

I didn't even know if she could respond, if she could hear me. She took in a deep breath that rattled her lungs. "Jahanara."

I nodded, then turned and stepped through the portal.

BRIBING DEATH

The Goblin Market was as far from orderly as one could get. It appeared to exist in an underground cavern so deep that the light from the gas lamps and torches that illuminated the market could not reach the ceiling. The market itself looked as though it were made up of any number of circus tents, semi-permanent wooden buildings, wagons drawn by horses and unicorns and monsters. I even spotted a hut that walked about on chicken legs, which did not appear to follow any laws of physics that I knew.

The air was permeated with noises, too. People haggled over wares in a hundred different tongues. Cages held creatures of the both mortal and magical varieties, making their displeasure at being caged well known. There was the sizzle of cooking meat, the sound of street musicians and buskers plying their talents. All of it faded together to become reminiscent of the largest of mortal cities, minus the noise of motorised vehicles.

And the smells! There was the damp of the cave, the sting of wood smoke, the aroma of a thousand different foods, the smell of unwashed people, of the creatures that were packed in here, and a distinctly magical tinge that burned my nose.

It was a living market, one of magic and a place where wonder could easily be found.

I could not bring myself to feel anything about it whatsoever.

"Now, we simply require some Fae food?" I asked, my voice pitched louder than usual so that Samuel could hear me over the hum of the market. He looked at me with that half-smile that showed too many teeth and did not reach the eyes, and I knew I had been deceived. Life laughed in my ear. I turned to glare at her and saw that she seemed to have grown taller, her ever-changing visage more turbulent, as if there was enough life energy here to increase her potency. Indeed, I felt my own Death-given powers rising as well, as if responding to the inherent magic in the air, the pervasive feeling that, while people here bargained for everything, the price might very well be their lives.

"Cal, you need to relax! Live a little," Life said, twitching her hips and clapping her hands in time to the music from a nearby camp of wagons. "Surely you wouldn't waste your time here?"

"We must find the food so that we can get back to the girl and get on our way," I said, stating facts. Life stopped dancing and rolled her eyes. She wandered a few feet away, glancing over a tiny, ramshackle stall displaying a number of brightly coloured scarves. Samuel, on the other hand, stepped closer to me.

"It's not just Fae food…" he said. I felt the urge to frown, so I did, though no more emotion came in accompaniment. Samuel licked his lips and glanced around as though nervous someone might overhear. Indeed, several creatures seemed to be watching, but I stared at them and they backed away, eyeing the shadowy wisps swirling around me with open fear. I turned back to Samuel.

"Please explain to me exactly what we need to do to get this cure," I said, a simple request for information. Samuel eyed me, a hint of his earlier, mischievous personality shining through. I waited.

"When a child is replaced by a changeling, they are taken to Faerie, where they are bound to a court and made to serve. The binding takes place by means of feeding them a very particular sort of food, made from the flowers that only grow in the magic of Faerie," Samuel said. He hunched his shoulders. "The problem is that the flowers are highly addictive, especially to humans. Once eaten, the child lives in eager service in the hopes that they will have more of the flower. I rescued her after the Fae had fed her the flower cakes."

"So she is suffering from withdrawal," I said. A tiny gremlin shuffled forwards and examined my shoe. I coughed and it looked up, flashing pointed teeth at me.

"I can fix the scratches, make it like new," it said, its voice deeper than I would have expected, given its size.

"The scratches are irrelevant," I said. "It would be illogical to care about the scratches on my shoes when

I can easily have them fixed at home. Also, it is likely that they will become more scratched during my time in the Goblin Market, so I would not bother to fix them, now, even I were inclined to such a thing."

The gremlin hissed at me and shuffled away.

I turned back to Samuel, who watched me with a smirk. "I haven't used logic to avoid bargains with market-goers before."

"Back to the issue at hand," I said, finding it rather pointless to discuss bargaining techniques with the man at that moment, simply because there would be no need for bargaining. We were here for one particular purpose, not a stop-and-shop. "We must acquire more of the flower cakes so Jahanara can manage her addiction."

Samuel stiffened, eyes widening. "How do you know her name?" he demanded, reaching out and grabbing the lapel of my suit jacket. "Did you *steal* it?"

I brushed his hands away, willing some of the shadows that wreathed around me to bite into his skin. He hissed and pulled back, waving his hands about to dispel the shadows. "I asked her what her name was. It seemed unusual to go about on a rescue mission for a girl whose very name I do not know. How would I refer to her if the linguistic occasion arose where using a simple pronoun would not suffice?"

"Names have power, Cal," Life said, finally deciding to reinsert herself into the conversation. She bore a scarf around her neck in a garish purple; the creature manning the shack stared at Life, swooning. I had no doubt the creature was the loser in that particular bargain. Life placed her arm on my shoulder. "For a child stolen from Faerie—even if they did steal her first—names have a very great deal of power. Especially given from the girl's own lips."

"What use have I for such things?" I scoffed. "She already has a bargain with Death. Holding more power over her would be pointless."

Samuel stared at me, the remnants of anger still present in the flaring of his nostrils, the tightness around his eyes. Once again, Life decided to step in and prevent this digression from taking up more time. "Relax, my dear Samuel. Cal, as ignorant as he is, truly does not have a malicious bone in his body. Nor is he scheming. He truly does not care about such things. Your child's name is safe with him."

In answer to this perfectly logical explanation, for which I silently applauded Life, Samuel jabbed me in the shoulder with a finger. "Do not use her name again while we are in the market."

"Very well," I said. "Now, if you would please continue explaining what it is that we need to find to curb her addiction?"

The wayward champion of Life closed his eyes and took a deep breath through his nose. I recognised this act from the behaviour of an old girlfriend who was fond of meditation. She often did this when she claimed that I had done something particularly exasperating.

"We cannot curb the addiction. She will devour all the cakes in an instant if presented to her and we will never find enough to sustain her over her life. No, she… pines away for loss of the flowers. We need to find an antidote, something that acts as the antithesis to Faerie power." Samuel hunched his shoulders again, looking around at the various tents and merchants of the Goblin Market. He did not look pleased.

"We need to find the Iron Witch," Life said, as if that meant anything more to me than Samuel's explanation had.

"Very well," I said again. "Where do we find this Iron Witch?"

Life grinned, showing her teeth, as if I had said something particularly invigorating or fantastical. Samuel just closed his eyes and took another one of those deep, meditative breaths. Then, Life slipped her arm through mine and started leading me through the Goblin Market. She offered no explanation as to our destination or the specifics of why we needed to seek out the Iron Witch. To be fair, I did not ask, as the current situation did not require such knowledge. I only needed to know that we were heading towards our destination and—

And what was that smell?

I lifted my nose, drawing in deep breaths to try to isolate that wonderful, pungent smell. It seemed to come from a small alley that was situated between a behemoth of a building made of wood and stretching an impossible number of crooked stories into the darkness of the cavern, and a brightly coloured circus tent embroidered with dancing deer and stars. I spotted the tiny kiosk—a two-wheeled cart with a single pot over a flame, and a few metal cups on the side—and disentangled myself from Life's arm to make a beeline for the wonderful aroma.

"Coffee," I said, my voice coming out a little strangled and two tones higher than normal. I took in another deep breath, recognising a superb roast. "Wonderful, wonderful coffee."

"Cal?" Life snapped, stalking up to me. She spotted the kiosk and groaned. Samuel stepped up to my other side and frowned.

"We don't have time for this," he said, grabbing my wrist and attempting to drag me away

"We *always* have time for coffee," I snapped, pulling my wrist free and shuffling as close to the kiosk as possible.

"Ah, an intelligent customer!" The owner of the kiosk appeared as if out of thin air and I actually recognised her species: a brownie. Though, where brownies were usually diminutive and possessed of large ears, an abundance of hair in all different colours, and a subservient attitude, this one had only one ear, and that a normal sized one, her hair was limited to a wild mane of dark curls on her head and her subservient attitude was more saucy than "how may I help you." I liked her immediately.

"You're selling coffee?" I asked hopefully. I shuffled my feet closer to the kiosk, though I really couldn't get any closer.

The brownie beamed at me, full of interest. "Not just *any* coffee! This is a Sumatran dark roast with a hint of cinnamon that has been imbued with brownie magic for an extra energy boost. It's *guaranteed* to give you that extra oomph you need."

"And it tastes good?" I bobbed my head eagerly, practically salivating at the anticipation.

"Cal!" Life whacked me over the back of the head. I rubbed the spot and ignored her. She hissed and turned to Samuel. "He has this… thing where he gets overly invested in any thought or mention of coffee. We won't get any use out of him until he's got a cup."

"There's nothing wrong with being invested in coffee," the brownie woman said with a sniff, looking down her nose at Life, who huffed in response. "My beans are by far the best coffee you will find this side of Elsewhere."

"Can I… can I get a cup?" I brushed my fingers over the side of one of the metal cups, putting on my most hopeful expression.

The brownie reached up and patted my cheek, beaming wider. "Of course you can, my love, provided you can pay for it?"

My face fell, and I hurriedly patted my pockets. The orb with the souls was not a possible source of payment. Nor was I carrying a wallet; in fact, I hadn't carried a wallet since signing on with Death. It hadn't really seemed necessary. I had my phone, which was turned off and which I hadn't thought of in at least two days, but there was nothing else except a handkerchief. I looked back up at the brownie, desperation making my throat tight.

"I, um, don't have any money," I murmured. The brownie scowled and folded her arms. She wasn't going to give me any coffee. I felt my heart breaking, and I desperately searched my mind for a solution, *something* I could offer her that she needed that would get me a cup of coffee.

"Look, if you don't have a means of paying—" she started, already backing away.

"No! I can pay through services!" I blurted, gripping the edge of the kiosk as if she might take it away from me. "I do marketing for Death and a few other clients and I would happily do marketing for your coffee business if you please, please, please give me a cup of coffee!" I spoke the words in a hurry, barely putting any space between them. In return, the brownie seemed to take far too long considering my offer. She stood there, tapping a foot, her arms crossed. Beside her, the coffee pot kept producing those wonderful smells. I inhaled deeply.

"Is he serious?" the brownie finally asked Life. "He does marketing for Death?"

I turned on Life and fixed her with my best pleading look. She heaved a dramatic sigh and tossed one end of her purple scarf over her shoulder. "Unfortunately, he speaks the truth. He does do marketing for my husband and several other entities within Elsewhere. And, I believe, that he would happily market your coffee. He probably wouldn't even foist it off on his assistants."

The brownie turned back to me. She glanced towards the coffee pot and then back at me. "Okay, fine. All the coffee you want in exchange for marketing."

She held out her hand. I took it eagerly and shook her so hard that she fell off the stool she was standing on. A moment later her head popped back up and she started pouring me a cup of coffee. I wrote down my contact information, social media links and address to be sure that she could find me, my hand moving so quickly that I'm sure the words were hardly legible. But she took the paper and handed me a cup of the most wonderful liquid in the entire world.

I took a sip.

Flavour burst onto my tongue, bitter and sharp and marvellous. It was perfectly warm without being scalding and went down my throat like liquid gold. There was an aftertaste of cinnamon, just as promised, and even as I took another sip I could feel energy settling itself into my limbs, making the shakes go away, the world turning into something better than it had been a moment before.

"Wow," I breathed, opening my eyes. My glasses were fogged from the drink. And, to my dismay, the kiosk and its owner were gone. I whirled around, careful not to spill a single drop of coffee. Both the building and the tent were still there, as were Life and Samuel. But the kiosk, the coffee seller, they were gone.

My heart shattered.

I took another sip of coffee and the world was alright again.

Besides, she would be contacting me for marketing, which meant I could probably figure out a way to get more coffee.

I sighed, a feeling of contentment spreading to my

limbs and tingling in my fingers. I smiled at Life and Samuel. "I love coffee," I informed them.

"We can see that," Samuel said, his voice dry. Life coughed into her hand. I thought about offering her a sip of my coffee to soothe her throat, but decided that I had better not. Who knew how long it would be until my next cup.

I sipped at the liquid again.

"Can we get on with finding the Iron Witch?" Samuel asked, whatever good humour he possessed already falling away. Some people had no appreciation for the finer things.

I opened my mouth to inform these two of exactly that when suddenly, the tent beside us flattened in a gust of impossible wind. The building let out a screech of terror and skittered away on legs that it could not have possibly had a moment ago. From inside, I could hear screams and shouts of alarm from the inhabitants. A few seconds later and it, too, was gone.

The three of us stood in the middle of an impossibly open space, considering how crowded the Goblin Market was. The ground was trampled earth, solid and unmoving, and yet it trembled beneath the leather slippers of the person who was approaching us. I moved to study her more closely, bringing my coffee once more to my lips.

If I expected the wondrous thing that was coffee to make my impression of this new person more favourable, then I was mistaken. Not even coffee could fix something like this.

She was old, the wrinkles in her skin deep and

brittle and the colour of sand. Her figure was hunched and twisted, like someone had taken an ancient olive tree and turned it human. Her hair was silver and red, sticking out from her head in impossible shapes. Her eyes were lidless, pewter grey orbs that rasped when she looked somewhere. Her mouth was lipless and revealed a set of iron teeth filed into points.

She flicked a finger at me and the half-full cup of coffee in my hand flew away, spilling its contents into the thirsty ground. She laughed, stepping forwards once more so that the earth trembled again.

"You spilled my coffee," I said, my words rasping in my throat.

"I did," she purred, her teeth clacking together as she spoke, sparking the way metal on metal does. "What are you going to do about it?"

I didn't think, didn't work through the logic of my actions. I just reached down into the power that Death had bestowed upon me and called it up, letting the indefatigable pull and the inevitable end rise in me. The shadows that had followed me around since taking this power surged around me, covering my skin in an armour that felt alive, burning with the knowledge that everything would come to me in the end. I might not have been true Death, but in that moment, I was close enough.

She had *spilled* my *coffee*. And she was going to pay.

EVERYONE DIES

The Iron Witch—because, really, who else could this be—cackled merrily at my transformation. "Oh, it has been *so* long since I've had to show a demon its proper place in the world," she said, dancing in place so that the ground shook beneath her leather slippers.

I flexed my hands into fists, opening them again and feeling the surge of power as the shadows moved around them. "I am not a demon," I snapped. "And you will pay for my coffee!"

The witch giggled, the sound incongruously girlish given her apparent age. She stepped forwards and raised a hand, directing some invisible power towards me. I couldn't see it, but I felt it easily enough. It was like a wind that blew in a single pointed spot, a lance that would have impaled me had I been a normal person. I was far from normal.

I raised my hand in return and the shadows leapt from my hand to create a barrier that stopped the witch's lance in its tracks. She frowned and dug her heel into the earth. "Not a demon?" she said, eyes sparking with interest. "Some sort of Fae, then. Foolish creature to come seeking after *me*."

She lowered her hands towards the ground, raising them up again. With her movements, specs of earth began to move as well. There were only a few particles at first, then more and more. Each time she lowered and raised her hands, rusty-red particles coalesced together until there were three spheres floating in the air, made out of metal that became more polished, more pure with each rotation.

"Is that meant to scare me?" I asked, taking a step forwards. She had ruined what was probably one of the best cups of coffee that I had ever tasted and I was tired of waiting for her to act. I took another step forwards and the witch retaliated with some sort of martial arts movement. The spheres barrelled towards me.

I saw no point in trying to duck out of the way. For one, I wasn't fast enough, and two, I had no real need for self-preservation. I *did* have a need for revenge and I was going to get it. The spheres—balls of iron, I realised—hit me like bullets, each one impacting me in a fatal spot. One went to my heart, another to my spine and a third to the centre of my forehead. They all impacted relatively simultaneously, their momentum throwing me back even as my body died and then returned. And when I returned, I was no less frustrated and angry than before.

Only, this time, I dived deep into Death's powers and grinned in feral pleasure as the witch faltered a step. "I'm no Faerie," I snarled. "And you cannot escape me."

She clacked her iron teeth, the sound like knife blades meeting. "Fae beastie, demon or Elderkin, I don't care. You are an insolent guppy, to think to call on *me* and draw *me* out for your own purposes. I am no mewling servant to be summoned! I am one of the nine witches! I will see you with your throat torn out."

"You *spilled* my coffee," was my response. In hindsight, there were a hundred different things I could have said that would have ended things before they began. I could have explained who I was, what sort of power I bore, even the fact that I couldn't die. But the loss of my coffee was the only thing on my mind. So we both flew forwards and clashed like titans raging over scorched earth.

The witch was strong, her body slamming into mine like a train, her teeth gnashing towards my throat. I pushed against her with everything I had, both my own strength and that loaned to me by Death. Her powers pushed back against me, preventing me from landing my own blows. I could only struggle against her as we crashed to the ground, ploughing a furrow in the earth and both of us getting numerous cuts and bruises as we tore at the other.

I fought harder, straining every muscle I had against the power that she held while she clawed at me with her nails, her teeth moving closer and closer to me, the shadows that strove against her barely keeping her away. She raised a hand high, bringing it down to rake her nails across my face. The shadows wrapped around her wrist, pulling her arm back and putting strain on her shoulder. Her power lanced towards me again, another pointed burst of pressurised air, strong enough to pierce my right shoulder and pin me to the ground.

I snarled, hardly feeling the pain.

We pushed back and forth, each of us gaining a single blow against the other while we fought off ten others. Our wills strained against the magical barriers holding us apart while we tried to keep the other away. And then, I felt a chink in her barrier.

I pulled my injured shoulder off the ground, wrenching my hips sideways enough to throw her off of me. It was one of the few moves that Agravane had taught me in the past few days. It was the only one he said he would trust me with until I could stop flailing my fists around like an octopus. It did the trick.

The witch staggered back, her weight working against her so that she fell backwards. In a flurry of motion I'm fairly certain I couldn't repeat, I was on my feet and kicking her so that she lay on the ground and I knelt above her. Then, I put my hand on her head.

The witch let out a choking breath, pewter eyes widening. "What is *this*?" she wheezed.

"It's Death," I said. "Or, at least, what power he loaned me while he's on holiday. It turns out, I don't need you to be already near death to capture your essence, drain you of life."

The witch flailed beneath me. Her movements became jerky, uncontrolled. She sucked in desperate breaths. I could feel her energy draining into me, and it was *glorious*. I threw my head back, savouring the power that surged into me. It wasn't just using me as a conduit, either, on its way to the orb. I wasn't in contact with the orb and this time, the power was flowing directly into me. It was like a jolt of adrenaline to the heart.

I could do *anything* with this power and not even Life herself could stop me.

"Cal."

I frowned. The witch still thrashed beneath me, her power still flowing through our joined skin. She hadn't spoken my name.

"Cal, you idiot."

I lifted my head and saw Life glaring down at me with her hands on her hips. Her ever-changing eyes were whirling faster than ever. Samuel cowered at her side, the mischievous imp now a whimpering man. I furrowed my brow, but did not remove my hand. The power was still flowing; how could I stop, now?

Life stalked closer, her hips sashaying with all the drama that she possessed. She folded her arms. "How is draining the Iron witch of her power the logical course of action when we *need* her to provide us with the girl's cure?"

Logical course of action?

What was she…

"Ah," I said, removing my hand from the witch's forehead. She sucked in a desperate breath, her eyes watering as she tried to pull back the essence that I had stolen from her. I closed my eyes and reversed the effect, knowing that it would be impossible for her to help us if she was half-dead. As logical a course of action as it was, siphoning the witch's essence back into her felt physically draining.

Or perhaps that was just my flaring emotions settling back down beneath the surface, returning to my standard non-emotional, logical, soulless state. It was not relevant, whichever the truth was. What was relevant was that the Iron Witch was sitting up, rubbing her chest and glaring at me.

"I do apologise for my, ah, associate," Life said with a sweeping hand to, I suspect, indicate me. "He has been having a few stability issues, especially in regards to a certain caffeinated beverage that I cannot mention by name for fear of starting him off again. Unfortunately, my husband has gone on holiday and left Cal in charge of his domain while absent."

"What?" the Iron Witch rasped, furrowing her brow and looking between the three of us. Samuel took a deep breath and stroked his beard.

"This is Life," he said, pointing to the entity in question. "That is Cal, an employee of Death."

"What do you want with me?" the witch snapped, rising to her feet and backing away. "An apology for spilling your—"

"No!" Life cut in, smiling and infusing the air with her power. I waved it away. The most important thing now was to garner the cooperation of the witch in procuring a cure for Jahanara. I was not the prudent choice for that, so I remained silent. "No," Life said again, smiling seductively. The witch narrowed her eyes.

"Don't you try any of that nonsense with me," she snapped. "I've been overlooked by you and your ilk for centuries. At least *he* was honest about his actions, even if they were ridiculous."

"We came to ask for your *help*," Samuel said, his tone perilously close to begging. From the expressions fluctuating over the face of this witch, I could see quite plainly that she either did not believe us, that she did not care, or that she had no intention of helping us, regardless.

I straightened the hem of my jacket, wondering how to clean dirt and bloodstains out of a wool-silk blend.

"Help?" The witch scoffed, tossing her head back so that the glow of the Goblin Market gas lights reflected off her teeth. "Why in the name of Elsewhere would I help *you*? Especially after you attacked me."

"Point of fact," I said, my voice flat and calm. The witch frowned deeply at me, the wrinkles at the corners of her mouth deepening. "My attack on you was not directly correlated to the fact that we sought your assistance, but in response to the actions you took in spilling my drink."

She stared at me, jaw dropping. "You're serious?" she asked. She looked between Life, Samuel and myself. "Tell me he's not serious."

Life chuckled. "He is perfectly serious. And he's right, too. In the traditions of Elsewhere, we are still allowed to bargain for your assistance. You attacked Cal. And for a completely different reason than why we are here. You know the laws, witch."

The witch gnashed her teeth, making a horrendous sound. Samuel winced. Life sighed. I simply stood there. "This is why I gave up dealings with your kind hundreds of years ago," she ground out. "Humans are far stupider and far less duplicitous."

"I am human," I pointed out so she could see the flaw in her logic. The witch froze, her movements turning into the preternatural stillness often exhibited by magical predators. Her eyes tracked me, though I did not move. No one said anything for a moment. It seemed as though the very air of the Goblin Market was holding its breath, waiting for one of us to make a move. I was not certain as to which course would be the best: asking the witch for her assistance; capturing her and invoking her assistance in exchange for her freedom; or seeking an alternative cure for Jahanara's illness.

Samuel, it seemed, had a different answer.

He sank to his knees and started drawing in the dirt, chanting in a strange language. I listened to identify the words, but my knowledge of human languages was limited and I had absolutely no knowledge of the tongues of Elsewhere. Most beings I interacted with spoke some form of English—or they had spells to approximate English. Yolanda had learned English from a correspondence course and her usage was accordingly poor. I had hardly bothered with languages except to learn how to accurately pronounce my clients' names. As such, I had no idea what Samuel was saying, or trying to do.

However, the witch seemed to know. And she did not appear to approve.

She straightened her shoulders, her expression flashing overt outrage. She clenched her hands into fists and let out a shriek, particles of iron—including the three spheres that had passed through me only a few minutes earlier—rising into the air. Samuel kept chanting.

"You *dare* invoke the old ways against me, mortal?" the Iron witch screeched. She raised her hands, drawing the iron together into one larger needle-like object, then waved her hands to send it towards Samuel. As he was, in fact, imminently mortal now, I would have to collect his soul when he died, no matter our agreement to save his family member. As I had already made the agreement to "fight" for the girl's life rather than her death, it seemed logical that I assist Samuel in doing just that.

I stepped in front of Samuel, taking the needle to my sternum. It hurt. A lot. But one of the things that I have discovered is that physical pain is quite simple to push aside when it is not bound to emotions. Yes, I still felt the pain. Yes, I would still have to deal with whatever damage the needle did—it pierced my bone and possibly entered a lung, but I was still standing and had not entered the white-flash of my not-death so I was confident that I would be able to continue assisting. But without fear and horror and anger to accompany the physical sensation, the pain was relatively easy to ignore.

So I ignored it.

Behind me, Samuel kept chanting, the words growing faster and more fervent. On the ground, lines of light began to etch themselves into the earth in a pattern that was intricate, beautiful, and completely unfamiliar.

The witch let out another scream. She flexed her hands and the needle began to move around inside me, a most uncomfortable sensation.

"Life," I said, my breath wheezing and confirming my suspicion that one of my lungs had been punctured. "You wouldn't be able to, ah, step in?"

Life cackled, circling around our little tableau as if it were simply entertainment. A show she could enjoy. "You should know better than that, Cal!" Life crowed. Samuel chanted louder. "I can accompany you, talk with you, even laugh at your mistakes, but I don't interfere."

I choked in a breath, coughing and wincing as the needle wended its way through what I think was my kidney. My vision grew spotty, telling me that my physical limits had almost been reached even if I was not dead. "You… interfered… plenty back in the mortal realm," I rasped.

"A shove to spill someone's soup? A nudge to wreck their car?" Life sneered. "None of those were events that changed the course of a person's life. A nudge, a whisper, a hint, all things that mortals experience on a day-to-day basis from a hundred different sources. None of them force a person to choose something—"

"A little less lecture, a little more brevity," I interrupted. My ability to help Samuel, still prone and chanting, the lines spreading more rapidly around the witch, was limited to how long I could remain conscious. Logically, that meant Life needed to get to the point.

She huffed. "I do not interfere in events that may change the course of a person's existence. Only mortals can do that. They can *choose*."

Oh. Ah. Interesting.

Life was fickle. Chaotic. Energetic. Cruel. Wondrous. Beautiful. Kind. Unfair. A thousand different things. But if what she said was true—and I had no reason to doubt her—then she couldn't actually interfere in the choices a mortal made that shaped their existence. She could place obstacles in their way. She could whisper. She could hint. She could even offer. But she couldn't actually force events into happening.

No wonder she was so entranced with mortals who chose to fight her. Who chose to live on their terms. They had the ability to choose. Life did not.

The black spots around my vision increased and my ability to draw in air lessened dramatically. The needle was somewhere in my right thigh, seeking a way out. The witch focused her wrath on it, knowing it was her best weapon to use against Samuel as he kept chanting, calling those lines in the earth. Whatever his magic was, it was binding her. Whatever her magic was, it could only affect iron directly. She pulled at the needle and it burst from my leg in a spurt of blood, which was *definitely* not coming out of my suit.

My vision flashed white just as my leg collapsed beneath me. I fell to the ground and became aware again only as my face hit the dirt, my glasses flying off into the distance. The damage that had been done by the needle had healed with my death, though I still ached in several places. And, more than that, I saw the witch in the centre of Samuel's etching, screaming and unable to move.

"Bound in blood, bound in pain, bound until boon is paid," Samuel croaked, this time in his usual accented English. Sweat poured down his face, making his hair and beard lank. His neck strained and the yellow pulsing that constantly surrounded him grew stronger. Whatever he was doing, he was pushing himself very, very close to death.

I licked my lips as I reached for my glasses, the urge to take his soul rising in me. The moment of pleasure would be brief, would be magnificent. I needed it.

I shoved my glasses on my face and climbed to my feet, nearly staggering over to Samuel. My feet hit the edge of the barrier and I was suddenly unable to move. I turned and looked at the etchings on the ground, forming a circle around both me and the witch. She was in the centre, unable to move beyond that, but I was in the outer ring, just as trapped.

I had stepped in front of Samuel to protect him and had unwittingly got tangled up in his binding spell. Which meant I could not reach out and pluck his soul from him.

I let out a hiss of rage and slammed my fist against the invisible barrier. A moment later and the rage was gone, replaced by emptiness. "Was binding me, too, intentional?" I asked, my voice not carrying even a monotone, heightened by rationality, but quiet and flat and void of anything.

Samuel looked up at me, his hands trembling in his lap. He was growing weaker from maintaining the binding spell with two of us inside. I did not have the knowledge to fight the spell with anything other than physical power, but I imagine the witch was doing everything she could to worm her way out of this.

"Not at first," Samuel said, licking his dry lips. He was growing pale, his normally healthy brown skin looking older by the moment. "But now it seems like it was a smart idea."

"I do not intend to hurt you," I said. "We had an agreement."

Samuel scoffed, the sound like a deflating bellows. "I don't think intent has anything to do with your actions, Cal. You will do what your nature demands that you do. You just have to ask what your nature *is*."

I considered his words. They were not, under the circumstances, inaccurate. I was currently obligated to perform Death's duty, which made my actions more inclined towards Death's nature than otherwise. Not to mention my lack of soul made things a little uncertain in the motive department; I was unable to access the parts of me that determined motive, but it was obviously still present or I would have simply taken Samuel's soul along with Jahanara's. The question was: what were my motives?

I did not have an answer.

"Stop your blathering and let me out," the witch crooned. I turned to her and saw that she was sagging under the strain of the binding. Her shoulders were hunched and the lines in her face more from weariness than anger. Samuel's will and magic, whatever it was, appeared to be stronger than hers.

"Not until you agree to provide a boon," Samuel said. He swallowed and wiped away sweat from his forehead. "Swear it."

"Of course I'll provide a boon," the witch said, her voice still unusually docile and sweet.

"*Swear it!*" Samuel shouted. Even I flinched at the power in his words. From beyond the circle, I could see Life prowling like some massive predator, grinning as she watched. I thought I saw an extra gleam in her eye, but a moment later and it was gone. The hackles on the back of my neck went up, though I had no particular reason to experience that sensation. Even while my thoughts ran rational and smooth, my instincts remained aware.

"I swear on the core of my power," the witch spat. I turned my attention back to her and saw venom in her gaze. She watched me just as much as she watched Samuel.

"And you, Cal," Samuel said, his shoulders sagging.

"I beg your pardon?"

"I bound you, too. I won't release it until you swear to provide a boon," Samuel said. His breath was beginning to come in short gasps and the yellow nimbus of his impending death was almost gold.

"Agreeing to save your family member isn't enough?" I asked. Life smiled wider, stepping closer to Samuel.

"Not now that I've bound you," Samuel wheezed. The same glint that had appeared in Life's eyes now shone in Samuel's. I understood, suddenly, what had happened. This wasn't planned. It wasn't forced. It was merely the seizing of an opportunity. A mortal's choice that might change the course of his life.

I wasn't the mortal to whom Life was referring.

Samuel was.

And the only boon I could possibly offer him was to not collect his soul as my duty to Death demanded.

CHEATING DEATH

"Swear it," Samuel said again, grinning despite his obvious weariness. I wondered, briefly, if I could wait him out. Eventually, the binding would break down simply because he was too tired. He was human, despite his magical workings. Likely he had picked up some wizardly arts during his centuries alive. But behind me, the witch was growing increasingly worn, too. I could see a yellow nimbus starting to form around her and knew that if Samuel kept her bound, eventually she would die. I wasn't being drained like she was because I hadn't been the target of the binding, just an unintended victim.

"You don't have a choice, Cal," Life crooned, standing over Samuel's shoulder like a proud parent.

"I thought mortals all had a choice. Isn't that why you love them so much?" I asked, drawing out the moment even if I was aware of the inevitable.

"Face it, Cal. You're not as mortal as you once were," Life replied.

She was not wrong.

I had Death's powers surging through my veins. I had the shadows of the inevitable flowing around me, drawing all people towards me. I was the unavoidable fact, even if only temporarily, and I had been outsmarted by a man who had held Life's favour for a time. I knew that I was human, too, and therefore prone to mistakes, but the reality of the situation rankled, a burr in my chest.

"Swear it!" Samuel demanded once more, slamming his fist on the ground.

"Do it," the witch hissed behind me. I turned and appraised her, seeing her yellow light growing stronger. If I let her die, I would be breaking my earlier promise to help Jahanara. That rankled more than being tricked.

"Very well," I said, my voice coming out in a hiss. "I swear to you one boon, in exchange for my freedom."

Samuel nodded, satisfied. Life chuckled, the sound turning into full-body laughter as I fixed my gaze on her. I did not know why I had agreed to help her, help Samuel, help Jahanara. None of it made sense or followed any logic that I could trace. Unless…

The binding started to come down and the witch immediately moved away from the centre of the circle, standing away from the fading lines in the earth. The golden glow around Samuel remained and I could have easily reached out and plucked his soul from him before he had a chance to ask for his boon. But I was too busy grasping desperately at a fact, a *truth* which had been dancing at the edge of my vision for some time, but which I hadn't understood.

I had thought that I had been acting rationally, along purely logical lines. But what if that assumption was simply a logical fallacy, a false assumption that coloured the rest of my actions? What if this Phantom Soul Syndrome was not making me fluctuate between hyperemotional states and states of hyperrationality. What if it was something else? Not emotion and logic, but strength of passion. Not no motive, but an unknowable one, hidden because the emotional under-currents weren't strong enough for me to read.

Something was guiding my actions. And I wasn't sure whether it was really me. Or rather, I wasn't sure whether the me before I lost my soul would have done the things that I was doing now.

"Coming to terms with your shift in reality?" Life smirked as she stepped up to me, a wicked gleam in her everchanging eyes. "You are a creature of Elsewhere, now, not some mewling human bound by mortal rules."

"I am human," I growled, trying to keep my voice quiet though I did not know why. "Still bound by human rules."

Life reached out and drew her hand along my face. It tingled, the power she held reacting badly with the power that flowed through me. And yet, I knew that had I been truly mortal—even unable to die—then I should have been burned by her touch. Life leaned close and purred in my ear, "I wouldn't be so sure."

I needed to get out of there. I needed to get back to

my office and talk with Yolanda, with Agravane, figure out just what was going on. I needed time to think, to process, to understand where I stood in the world, what my motivations truly were. What I *was*.

But in order to get out of there, I needed Life to return me to Elsewhere. She was unlikely to do that unless I helped her finish what we started. I had to work with Samuel to save Jahanara. I had to grant his boon.

Grinding my teeth together, I took a deep breath, forcing all my emotions to flow away with the exhale. I relaxed my muscles, felt my more reasonable and rational thoughts take over. I wasn't going to consider whether or not it was true rationality. I couldn't if I wanted to remain sane. I moved towards Samuel and the Iron witch.

"Finally decided to grace us with your presence?" the witch sneered. I regarded her cooly.

"My boon is not the one in question at this moment," I said. "Yours is."

She scowled, drew her hands closer to her chest, almost as if protecting herself. Then, she spat on the ground, the saliva landing nearly on my feet. Interesting that it was my feet and not Samuel's at which she aimed.

"Witch," Samuel said, an imperiousness to his voice that I hadn't ever heard before, "I collect on your sworn boon. Give to me an antidote for the addiction that affects my kin from when she was taken and replaced by a Faerie changeling."

The witch threw back her head and cackled, her

wild hair bouncing as she heaved in a breath and continued cackling. After a moment, her laughter subsided and she drew a finger under each eye, wiping away silver tears. "An antidote for Fae food? Oh, you are ambitious, aren't you?"

"That is the boon I require," Samuel snapped, voice hardening. His shoulders straightened, his hands clasped behind his back. He looked worse than when he was holding the binding together. Less contained.

The witch saw this, too, and she sneered at Samuel, her iron teeth flashing in the gas lamp light. "You understand what has happened to her? What was done when she ate of Faerie food?"

"They laced their food with something," Samuel sniffed. "Everyone knows that's why you don't eat Faerie food. Because it's addictive, because it makes you want more and you'll do anything to get it."

The witch looked at me as though we shared some private joke. I raised one eyebrow and she scoffed, turning away. "The food is not *laced* with anything, foolish human. It is simply *more*. More flavourful, more nutritious, more real than any food you could possibly contemplate. Why do you think that Fae who live in their realm in Elsewhere live so long and those that are outside do not? Why do you think there is a black alley in the Goblin Market to peddle such foods? The Fae are primal beings. You think them ephemeral, hard to pin down, which is why their magic is in glamour and light and shifts in reality. But the truth is that we are the ones who cannot fathom how truly *real* they are. We are the ones who are ephemeral." The witch leered at me and gave a mocking bow. "Some of us are more ephemeral than others."

I didn't know if she meant me or her, but it didn't really matter. I did look to Life to confirm the witch's story, as it didn't match anything that I'd ever heard before about Faeries or any of their kin. She just shrugged, which could have meant a thousand things, or it could have meant nothing. Again, it did not truly matter as we simply needed the antidote from the witch.

Samuel hissed through his teeth, whatever temper he had left at its end. He was still looking a bit peaky, which made the witch smile wider. I, myself, could see Samuel's soul clearly, a glowing being superimposed over his form. He was beyond the point of death; he probably should have died while trying to enact that binding. But I could not act to free him from that torment and to take his soul—delicious, powerful, tempting—through myself and into the orb.

Not yet, anyways.

"Just give me the antidote," Samuel said, sweat beading on his forehead.

The witch tsked, clicking her tongue and making a metallic sound against her teeth. "What you ask is not easy, human. You need something to unground your kin, to balance her with the mortal realms when her very soul wants to be where it felt all the more real."

"Give. Me. The. Antidote." He took a step closer to the witch, his chest nearly brushing hers. His hands were clenched at his side and he seemed completely unconcerned by the threat of the witch's metal teeth and claws. I would have been impressed at his stupidly courageous determination if he weren't also shivering, his body failing him.

I inhaled deeply and the soul overlaid on Samuel flicked me an uncertain glance.

"She needs something just as ephemeral, just as impossible as the mortal realm. Something which the Fae always crave, just as they always crave the unpredictable nature of humanity. True love would be a good one," the witch said, smiling and tapping her chin with a claw. She spotted the snarl building on Samuel's tongue and rolled her eyes. "Impossible to deliver, at this current moment, I know. But something equally ridiculous, an archetype, a trope, a story to be fulfilled, that will suffice nicely."

I didn't quite like the way that the witch was eyeing me.

"This doesn't make sense," I said, the words falling from my tongue before I could stop them. I wasn't sure why I had said them, either, only that they were true. Or at least, I knew them to be true, but I didn't know how I knew. I had very little personal experience with the Fae. The closest I had got was demanding back taxes from a fetch and his banshee wife. While they were Fae, and definitely had a specific nature, they were the mortal realm's versions of such legendary beings. They were mortal, closer to human than otherwise. And they didn't seem to have this... this... fundamental realness that the witch was talking about. But there was also something else, something more, that told me to press the issue. Maybe I should have questioned that thought, as every one I had at that point was suspect, but I didn't.

I pressed the issue, instead. "Nothing I've ever heard says that the Fae are so real as you claim, witch. In fact, I've heard just the opposite. Their natures are *unsolid*, a wisp of mist, a story."

The Iron Witch hissed at me, a sound of frustration and annoyance. "Yes, yes, people think the Faerie are inherently chaotic. Indeed, they do pursue chaos, but that is because they cannot create it on their own. They are bound to their natures. The Sidhe will always act as Sidhe, masters of their domains, just as the Seelie and the Unseelie courts will always work in opposition, in balance to the other. Darkness, light. Seasons, transitions. The callers of Death will always act as callers, just as the healers and benevolent ones will always act as healers and benevolent. They are firm, *fixed*, therefore more solid and real than beings such as you humans, who change at the slightest rise in the winds."

That definition of real seemed reasonable, I supposed. Something still itched at my mind, telling me that her explanation wasn't quite complete, that there was a piece missing. And then I remembered a word that she had mentioned. "Archetype," I said, frowning. The witch blinked, eyes flashing. "You said that letting his kin fulfil an archetype, a story, something that was fundamentally ephemeral, would be an antidote. But by your definition—"

"The Fae *are* archetypes," Samuel interrupted, catching my train of thought and turning his wrath upon the witch. He reached out those scant few inches separating them and wrapped his hand around her throat. "What are you trying to do, you fiend?!"

I frowned. "People really call each other fiends?"

Life appeared at my shoulder and draped an arm around my waist. "Cal, I think you've probably helped Samuel enough. Perhaps you should take a step back and remain quiet rather than commenting on people's vocabulary when it's not helpful?"

Indeed, it seemed that Samuel had a decent grasp on the situation, his fingers digging deep into the witch's neck so that she was spluttering, clawing at him. "My boon! I demanded my boon and *this* is how you repay me? With lies and tricks? You will be diminished by breaking your promise. I'll have your magic from your very bones!"

The soul flickering over Samuel's form gained strength, almost becoming more solid than its host. "I don't know how much longer I can resist taking his soul," I said to Life as we watched the two struggle. She sighed and nodded her head, resting her cheek against my shoulder. Her hair tingled where it touched my skin, but it did not burn.

"I know," she said, sounding melodramatically sad. "It will be such a shame to lose such a wonderful champion, but such is the way of things."

"You don't seem at all concerned," I countered. She lifted her eyes to look at me and then moved her gaze back to where Samuel was holding the witch, his grip undiminished and the rage in his eyes vibrant. Even as Life and I spoke, the two of them seemed to be moving in slow motion, the words forming on their lips sluggish and impossible to understand. It was as if the world had shifted because Life and I were having a conversation, as if our words were of more importance, more weight, than the events happening around us.

"Cal, one thing you still need to learn is that it is my nature to act in opposition to my husband's, just as the witch described the Fae. I can shift, change, be as fickle as I like, but that is simply my nature. No matter what I do, what *you* do, that is fact." Life lifted her head from my shoulder and smiled sadly at me, this time the emotion appearing genuine.

"I was more referring to the fact that Samuel still holds my boon. He's going to demand that I release him from his obligation to die," I pointed out. Samuel's soul looked at me, eyes wide, its movements appearing to happen in real time while Samuel and the witch moved ever slower. The soul quickly looked away.

Life nodded. "I had considered that. But you are not Death, no matter how much his power suits you. I don't think it would be possible for you to resist taking his soul, despite owing him a boon. No, there are some things that cannot be bargained for. And Samuel's death is one of those."

"Then..."

Life tightened her hand on my waist. "Then you obviously don't understand my nature. Or yours. Perhaps you should think on that before you speculate on such matters. There might be more at stake than you think."

I was going to respond, but the world seemed to

shift again and suddenly Samuel and the witch were moving as expected. Samuel's momentum and his grip around her throat allowed him to throw the witch to the ground and straddle her, his weight—no matter how slight—providing the pressure he needed to keep her down. In turn, the witch scrabbled at his arm with her claws, gouging deep lines in his flesh so that blood ran freely.

"Your false promise will be your undoing," Samuel said, foam flecking his beard.

The witch choked something out, something which I couldn't quite understand. Life, though, seemed to grasp the communication just fine. She swept forwards and stood at her champion's shoulder.

"If you give her a moment to explain, I think you'll find she hasn't broken her promise," Life said blandly, as if commenting on the weather. Samuel's head jerked back as if she had struck him and a moment later he had let the witch go. She was obviously still fuming, still out for Samuel's blood. She wiped away the liquid where it had flowed onto her face, eyes narrowed and suspicious.

"I'm not idiot enough to renege on a boon," the witch rasped, coughing twice. "It would mean the destruction of my powers, my life."

"Then *why* did you suggest—" Samuel started, clenching his injured hand into a fist. I winced on his behalf.

"Fool! Do you not understand? The Fae food has made her more grounded, more real, less changeable. Why do you think that the Fae deliver their children as changeling?" The witch bared her teeth, now speckled with red. It was not a charming sight. "To give them the ability to *change*. To maybe take some of that impossible humanity into them and evolve into something better. Something more adaptable. Above the prescribed order of things."

"What does that have to do with *my* family?" Samuel snapped, breathing as ragged as the witch's. She closed her eyes, swallowing and rubbing her throat.

I stepped in, some glimmer of understanding reaching me. "The Fae exchange their children for human children. Hoping to give them that life. In exchange, the humans must become… they become some sort of Fae. Don't they?"

The witch nodded. "It's not complete, since most humans are too weak to make a full transition. But those that do it? Those that complete the story or fulfil an archetype, they take on Fae persona. They become fully grounded, real."

I placed a hand on Samuel's shoulder, ostensibly as an act of comfort. Part of me—a loud part—knew that it was simply a ploy to try to touch Samuel's soul, which was now fully visible, as though two people were existing in the same place. Without touching his skin, though, my hand just slipped right through the soul. That power, that potential, lay just out of reach.

"Your… niece, she has to either become Fae or die."

Samuel didn't much care for my words. He jerked away and paced in a small line where that delightful kiosk once stood. But, no, I couldn't think of that right now. I had to focus. And coffee—No!

"Is that… the only option?" Samuel asked, voice shaking.

"No," the witch said, drawing both of our gazes. "But it is the only one that you could possibly accomplish soon enough for it to make a difference."

No one said anything for a moment. Life seemed to be wandering between Samuel, the witch, and myself. I just stood there, waiting. In fact, all of us seemed to be waiting. It was time for Samuel, the mortal amongst the immortal, the changeable one, to make his decision.

That single realisation seemed to push a weight onto my mind. I was no longer mortal. I might not have even been human. I was Other. Samuel, for all that he had lived several centuries, remained fully human, down to his right to make this decision. He was not bound by promises that could change your very being if you broke them. He was free in a way that I might never be again.

I think I hated him, just then.

If I did not, it didn't matter; the surge of emotion quickly passed. I simply waited for his decision.

"Okay," Samuel breathed, nodding his head. "What do I have to do?"

"There are many archetypes that a person can fulfil. True love is the most powerful, if impossibly difficult to find. The hero's journey is the most common. But to complete an archetype, a story, powerful enough to complete the transition, she must do something that is truly remarkable in her hero's journey. Slay a dragon, though I don't recommend that one. Solve a mystery, though that often requires a dead body. Save the world." Then, the witch looked straight at me, once again making me the focus of her plans, the solution to her problems. "Overcome Death."

Samuel spun to face me, eyes widening. "Yes," he breathed.

As soon as he said that word, the witch let out a piercing cackle, straight out of a B-rated Halloween movie, and vanished in a small cyclone. There remained only the three of us and an empty space in the Goblin Market. Already, the buildings that had retreated seemed to be inching back, the threat to their wellbeing gone. But that wasn't the important part, though watching a multi-storied wooden building scuttle closer on tiny legs was rather mesmerising to watch.

No, the important part was that Samuel was now looking at me like a predator looked at prey.

"Now what am I supposed to do?" I grumbled.

A SWIFT DEATH

{B}efore I had a chance to demand that Samuel clarify just what sort of scheme he had concocted from the witch's words, he rounded on Life. "Take us back," he said. Eyes wide, skin feverish, he looked as though he shouldn't be alive. The mere presence of his soul—obviously stubborn and determined—was keeping him alive. Most humans would have long since expired, likely just waiting for me to arrive and take them away.

Samuel was something else entirely.

Interesting.

Life lifted her chin. "Do you know what will happen when you get there?"

"Yes." He seemed so assured.

"No," I grumbled, sounding merely grumpy by comparison. "And since everyone was staring at me just a moment ago, I assume that I won't like whatever it is that we're going to do."

Life grinned, clapping her hands together gleefully.

I wanted to cuff her over the head, but doubted that would go over well. Though I doubted very much that Death would mind if I did so, even if I would have to explain upon his return. The thought of explaining the last few days to Death made me scowl deeper, which Life seemed to think indicated my distinct displeasure with her and only made her crow louder.

"Oh, goodie," she said, sounding like a small child. Then, she waved her hand and the rapidly shrinking open space that surrounded us wobbled, like water rippling when a stone was thrown. Solid ground should not do that.

I tried to stagger backwards, but whatever Life had done to the ground grabbed my feet and refused to let me go, the dirt climbing up my legs as though I were drowning. I managed a glare at Life before the ground swallowed the three of us and transported us back to the abandoned village in the mountains.

Life and Samuel, I noted as I fell to the ground and landed firmly on my behind, arrived gracefully, only a few particles of dirt clinging to their clothes. I had to brush soil and debris from my hair, my suit, and wipe my glasses thoroughly before I felt even remotely presentable. I was fairly certain that there was dirt in places I'd rather not mention. All thoughts of remaining logical and calm seemed to have vanished with the realisation that I wasn't what I thought I was. Instead, I was feeling distinctly put out. That emotion was rapidly rising towards anger.

I stood, brushing myself off. The shadows that had become my constant companions hummed around me, their vibrations almost like words mirroring my emotions. "You did that on purpose," I said to Life. She tossed her hair—a favourite move of hers, I noted—and sniffed.

"Well, naturally. Come, Cal, surely you wouldn't expect me to treat you like a normal person, now would you?" Life stepped forwards and drew her hands down the lapels of my jacket. She lowered her chin and looked up at me from beneath her lashes. "Now that you're *so close* to understanding, the normal rules don't apply to you."

"Understanding what?" I asked, my voice harsher than I would have expected, given how non-threatening Life was in that moment. She adjusted my pocket square.

"If I knew, that wouldn't make watching you figure it out so fascinating," was her whispered response. She pressed closer. "The offer still stands, you know. I can stabilise your condition, make it so you don't fluctuate between one extreme and the next. All you have to do is be my champion, work for me."

"Those are not the same things," I retorted, feeling my anger harden into the coolness of logic. Not emptiness, not anymore. Coldness. Fury, boiled down until there was nothing left but the quiet of rational thought. "Being your champion. Working for you. They are not the same thing. Not equal. Even if I were considering your offer, I would not be both. Never both."

I leaned closer to Life, my mouth an inch away from her ear. "Pick one."

She hissed and pulled back, my lost fury rippling

across her features. She pulled her shoulders back and spun away from me, turning her attention to Samuel. "Let's get on with this, shall we?"

He was standing at the head of Jahanara's bed, his hand resting on her forehead as if he could draw strength from himself and give it to her. Or as if he could draw strength from her for his own. I couldn't judge his expression or his intent properly, not with his soul so vivid over his features.

Jahanara, though, I could judge. She was still surrounded by a golden nimbus, brighter than before. Her breathing was laboured and she looked pained; being in this world was killing her, so I understood. She blinked once, her jaw working to ask a question never spoken.

"We have a solution," I said, though I don't know why.

Samuel knelt by his kin's bed, brushing strands of dark hair away from her face. "My child, we have a way for you to get better. But you won't... you must... you will become Fae."

Her eyes brightened at the mention of the Fae and she licked her lips. It seemed that the craving was strong, perhaps even as strong as the witch intimated, no matter that her words may very well have been lies. Not her solution—no, I trusted that she paid her boon honestly for fear of the consequences—but her explanation. It seemed... too easy.

"How?" Jahanara croaked. Samuel looked at me out of the corner of his eye. He must have seen something in my gaze that he didn't quite like, because he turned back to the girl and started whispering in her ear. I could probably have leaned closer and listened, but I was too busy watching the movements of his soul to pay attention to his words.

Jahanara shook her head weakly. Samuel tightened his fist, just as weakly, and spoke harsher words in her ear. Then, Life stepped to the foot of the girl's bed. "Do not fear, child. There will be no lasting damage for what you must do. Not to him."

"Not to him?" I asked, adjusting my glasses on my nose. "I don't particularly care for the sound of that."

"Relax, Cal," Life said with the particular tone of voice that was usually followed by a roll of the eyes. "You'll be fine."

"Why won't any of you tell me the plan?" I asked. I, too, stepped closer to the bed. Samuel gripped Jahanara's hand as her eyes flashed to me, wide and terrified. "I know the witch said something about overcoming death—and since I'm acting as Death, I'm sure you think that overcoming me is an acceptable solution—but is there a particular *type* of overcoming that you had in mind? After all, I've already agreed to help her, against my better judgement."

And how foolish an agreement it seemed, now. There she was, helpless, dying. Her body was mere inches away from death and then her soul would be just sitting there, ready for the taking. I would only have to reach out and touch her, taking her soul into me before it fled into the orb that held all of that magnificent power. Human souls. The essence of beings from Elsewhere. Energy that made an individual unique. It was full of such *potential*. Here was a girl who could do nothing to me if I decided to lean forwards and brush my hand against her forehead.

Indeed, I was only inches away from her. Somehow, I stood where Samuel had been. He had moved away from me, probably for the same reason that the girl now looked up at me with horror in her eyes. It was not unexpected, but it stung. Didn't they understand? I wasn't going to *hurt* her. I was simply going to release her from her pain. I was going to gather her soul, collect it for whatever came next.

I was not cruel.

But I was necessary.

I was Death, and this girl, Jahanara, she was ready for me.

I reached out to touch her, to move her hair back from her temple and to lay my fingers on her bare skin, to initiate the touch that would free her from her obvious agony. My hand got within centimetres from her skin when a sharp, desperate sensation flooded my chest.

I pulled back and looked down, staggering away from the bedside. A knife—a dull knife at that—protruded from my chest, the tip of the blade already tickling my heart. It *itched* and it hurt. I recognised this sort of pain and it wasn't the agonising, instantaneous death that I usually experienced and recovered from so quickly. I was bleeding out, all over my suit and my shoes. Well, at least I wouldn't have to go through the bother of trying to save it. There were just some things you couldn't clean out.

"That, dear Cal, is why we couldn't explain," Life said. She moved to my side and grabbed my arm, helping me into a chair while I watched my blood soak into the ground. I wrinkled my nose and looked up at her. "The threat from you had to be genuine."

"Great," I said drily. "So, what, she kills me and all is well?"

"She overcame Death," Life said. Life frowned, "Or, well, Death's proxy, which is good enough. As soon as you die, then her transformation can begin."

"Shouldn't be long now," I said as a familiar faintness came over me. I supposed that even a dull knife could have nicked the right artery for me to bleed out this quickly. At least I wasn't going to spend the next twenty minutes gasping like a fish out of water.

Jahanara was staring at me with that same horror as before. She hadn't been afraid of me, I realised, but of what she had to do. At least there were some small favours. I didn't want people to be afraid of me. "I'm sorry," she whispered. Her voice was already stronger than before, as if the very act of stabbing me had accomplished what we set out to fix.

"Don't be." I smiled at the girl. I wanted to pull the knife out, make all of this go faster, but I doubted that the onlookers would have appreciated that level of gore. So I left it in and waited for the whiteness to appear. "There are not many who have the strength to make such a choice."

Jahanara licked her lips, a wild gleam appearing in her eyes. They started to change, even as my own vision faded at the edges to whiteness. Her eyes grew larger, slanting, her facial structure shifting to become something that held all the beauty of an immortal predator. Her ears moved upwards slightly, the ends sharpening into points. She had a feral look about her and her teeth sharpened ever so slightly. "There was no choice," she hissed. "Only desire."

I blinked once more and the whiteness overcame me. I didn't get to see the last piece of Jahanara's transition; I wasn't going to complain. There was something disconcerting about watching the pieces of someone that were human transition into something that was not. Perhaps it was good that I was a being of Elsewhere, now. Those in the mortal realms wouldn't have to watch my own, slower, transition.

The whiteness filled my vision for longer than before. Only once had I been in the white for so long, and then, as now, there were faint whispers that met my ears. One of the whispers seemed louder than the others. It was urgent, desperate, distant. It was also wildly familiar, in a way that warmed my very being, filling me with more emotion than I had felt in a very long time.

"Cal." I opened my eyes to Life staring me down, her face too close, her pupils dilated and her breath warm on my face.

"Ugh," I said, though I don't know whether that was reflexive or a true reaction to the situation. Life huffed and pulled back, leaving me to sit up straight in the chair on my own.

"He's fine," she said, crossing her arms. "Jahanara, how do you feel?"

Before me, I saw what every young person wishes they could be. It was the human form, idealised. She had healthy, glowing golden-brown skin. Her hair was lustrous and black, shining down like a wave of night. Her eyes were large and brown, drawing you in. She *looked* like Jahanara, the young human that we had fought to save, but she also looked like more. She was Other, like me. And not like me.

She was Fae.

She fixed me with a knowing look and smiled, showing her pointed teeth. "I feel *wonderful*," she said, even her voice somehow more true, more tempting, more melodious. "It's like the power of the world is at my fingertips."

Life chuckled. "Very good, my dear. Now, say goodbye to your uncle before I take you to Faerie."

The newly formed Fae froze with preternatural stillness, her eyes fixed on Life. I saw a flash of a predatory gleam, then she frowned. "No," she said. "I don't want to leave."

"Figures," I grumbled, still a little wobbly from whatever I had felt in the beyond. "Do a favour and people still complain. Look, kid, I don't think you have much of a choice in the matter."

Defiantly, she lifted her chin, a fox staring down Life and Death. Or, well, Life and Death's proxy. I doubted that I made a terribly cutting figure at the moment. "You don't have any authority over me," she said with a particular assuredness that came from being young.

Life, to my surprise, was the one who responded.

She bared her teeth, a wolf's grin spreading across her features. Then, she took a step towards the girl. "Choice is for the mortals, *Fae* child. Immortal you may be, powerful, young, but you are now *bound* by your nature. And unless you want to give all of that up to remain in the mortal realms for the rest of your natural life, then you don't have a choice. You will go to Faerie."

Jahanara sucked in a breath and looked down at her hands. They were delicate, artistic, and just enough into the realm of perfection to be inhuman. But I watched, and as I did, a flash of brief light flared from the tips of her fingers and then vanished. It was yellow light. Her essence, draining away.

She stood in the mortal realms, I realised. And, like the fetch Dermot Green and his banshee wife Mathilde, power would be stripped from her until she was mortal again. Still Fae, still powerful, but mortal. The longer she remained, the worse off it would be, I imagined.

"Make it stop," Jahanara pleaded, lifting her gaze to mine, as if I would be the sympathetic one. To be fair, I probably would be, under normal circumstances. It was difficult giving up power, influence, opportunity. Even if she remained and was one of the peak people in the world of humans, it wouldn't be the same as the power she held now. Not all beings were like that. Vampires, for example, seemed to function the same on either side of the barrier between Elsewhere and the mortal realms. But Fae, apparently, did not.

"I can't," I said, voice somewhat cold. "And even if I could, I wouldn't. I don't believe that you are forever bound by your new nature, but you do have to make a decision. Stay here, or go to Faerie. Retain mortality and choose, or immortality and follow the path set before you."

The words, once again, didn't feel like my own though I instinctively knew them to be true. I blinked and swallowed, shoving down the sensation. When I refocused my gaze, Jahanara had her hands clenched into fists at her sides, her expression defiant and yet defeated. She knew she had lost this battle. She nodded, once. "I will go."

"My child," Samuel said, his voice a rasp. He was leaning on the edge of the bed, obviously exhausted. Frankly, I was surprised that he was still moving. He tracked Jahanara with his eyes, surrounded by sunken depths and shadows. He twitched a smile, barely, at her healthy form moving about the small room. "It will be okay."

Jahanara ignored him. She didn't look at him, acknowledge him, or even act as though he still existed. And, given the state of his person and his soul, perhaps he didn't exist on the same plane as she did any longer. She stepped swiftly past him, her movements already graceful and predatory, and extended a hand towards Life.

Life snickered in response. "One of the things you must learn, Fae child, is that there are beings far more powerful than yourself. You should not go about touching them."

Jahanara sucked in a breath through her nose, nostrils flaring, eyes flashing. I almost thought that she would reach out and take Life's hand, just for the sake of defying her. But something about the fundamental energy that flowed around Life must have stopped her. For a moment, she looked at me, seeing the shadows writhing around me. I returned her look, remembering just how close I had come to tasting her soul.

She shuddered and turned back towards Life. "I am ready, now," Jahanara announced, squaring her shoulders.

Life smirked. "I'm sure you think you are." She twisted towards the wall where we had stepped through to the Goblin Market and it began to shimmer. Another portal, this one producing sparks, appeared.

"Wait!" Samuel cried. Jahanara did not acknowledge him; she just stepped through the portal and Life followed after her. The portal flickered into nothingness, leaving Samuel and I alone in the hut.

Samuel collapsed on the bed, his hands trembling on his knees. "There was so much I wanted to tell her, about her family, about her history."

"I don't know that she cared," I said. Samuel Phipps glared defiantly at me, the sheer strength of emotion coming from his soul overpowering that of his human body. "You must know it was true. The reasons that you had for saving her were not the same as the reasons she had for accepting your help."

He shook his head. "I… I had *hoped…*," he breathed.

I managed to stand, my body recovered from being stabbed, and walked over to sit beside Samuel on the bed. I didn't offend him by reaching out a comforting hand. We both knew what that would really mean.

"One of the things I'm learning about being human is that maybe hope is a good enough cause."

"You, of all people, would say that to me?" Samuel snarled. "You *know* what is coming for me."

I sighed. "The way I see it, you have two options. One, you can collect on the boon that I owe you and demand I ignore your death. If you do that, though, there is no guarantee that Life will offer you the same deal as before. In fact, I think it really unlikely."

"What do *you* know of Life?" Samuel snorted. He reached up a trembling hand and rubbed his neck, flinching where his skin scraped against his beard. He soon lowered his hand again.

I tightened my own hand into a fist, more to prevent myself from blindly reaching out and taking his soul as I so desperately wanted to do. "A fair bit, actually. The real question is what *you* know of her. Think about it Samuel. In all your centuries of living, have you known Life to be consistently fair, good, kind, generous? Or is that side of her nature interspersed with things like greed, fickleness, cruelty, indifference, even disdain?"

Samuel licked his dry lips.

"She is stunning and wonderful and absolutely a pleasure to be around," I admitted, "but you can't expect her to be consistent. If you believe that you have a chance, demand that boon of me. But if you don't, then you'll wander around in the state you're currently in. Your soul will continue to try to break free of its bindings. You will be a shade of your former self. You won't be able to use what little magic you have. You'll struggle to do things like walking, talking. It won't be easy."

Samuel jerked his head in what I believe was meant to be a nod, though it looked more like a spasm. "Life is never *easy*," he rasped.

I smiled, gently, this time reaching out and placing my hand on his knee, careful not to touch any exposed skin. "No," I agreed. "And you would happily fight her for the rest of your days. That's the thing, Samuel; you may evade me for now, but the true Death? The Death that you expected to meet, he'll find you, eventually. You would only delay the inevitable, and for what? Your family is gone, you would be living in constant agony, you have lost Life's favour… what remains for you here?"

"You can't convince me to kill myself!" Samuel was gasping now, terrified of Death, as nearly everyone was.

"If there's just one truth I can offer you, then it's this: Death isn't the enemy. You don't need to seek him out; he'll be there. He is the release from your pain, the light in the shadows at the end of life. He's not the end of all things, just of this one piece of your existence."

"Liar. How can you know what lies beyond?" Samuel jerked his knee, and I removed my hand. His soul was straining against his skin, practically calling to me. I felt sweat bead on the back of my neck as I resisted the urge to capture Samuel's soul right then and there.

I closed my eyes and thought of the perpetual whiteness that I saw every time I died, every time I

came closer to the end of my existence. There was…
something there, calling me, watching me. I didn't know
what. I didn't know who. I didn't care.

"I have died many times," I said, keeping my eyes
closed as I focused on the memory of really feeling
things again. "Trust me, I know."

I opened my eyes and watched Samuel. He was
panting, struggling to catch enough air to fill his lungs.
His eyes were glazed, unfocused, and he swayed
slightly with every beat of his heart. His soul was
crying out in anguish, a sound so profound that I could
almost hear it. There was nothing more I could do to
persuade Samuel. In the end, as Life had said with jealousy sparking in her eyes, it was his choice.

Samuel extended a shaking hand. "My boon," he
ground out, "from you… make it swift."

An invisible barrier that had been holding me back
—the boon, I realised, still waiting to be enacted—
vanished. I nodded once, swiftly, and extended my
hand to take his.

Then, Samuel Phipps, champion of Life and a man I
found that I actually liked, died.

YOU ONLY DIE ONCE

Samuel's soul flowed into me with as much force as any of the others, but I could have sworn that it was richer, deeper. Stronger. Maybe it was the extra time that he had lived, though the essences of those beings from Elsewhere who had lived centuries didn't have quite that depth of flavour, of power, to them.

I threw my head back and closed my eyes, understanding somewhere in the back of my mind that I was acting like a drug addict desperate for my next fix. And what a fix it was. For a brief moment, while Samuel Phipps' soul shared my body, I was *whole* again. I wasn't confused about what I was feeling. I had an infinity of choices laid before me and any one I chose presented another infinity. I was brimming with potential. With power.

This was what I was missing. It was hard to understand just what sort of thing I had lost when Death released my soul until I was experiencing what it was to have one again. Not even my temporary bargain with Al Capone had felt so strong and true.

Then, just as I was beginning to relish in the opportunities and the possibilities laid before me, the feeling vanished. Samuel's soul joined the countless others in Death's orb, leaving me empty and unaware of the paths before me. The power and raw potential was gone. The sureness that what I felt was right and real, that was gone. All that was left was the shell of what I had once been. The emptiness warring with whatever shreds of feelings I had remaining warred within me. More often than not, the emptiness won.

I opened my eyes and lifted a hand to adjust my glasses. My fingers touched my cheek and came away damp. I trembled as I lowered my hand, already desperate for another fix. Samuel's dead face leered at me, his body slumped where it had fallen from the bed in the throes of death. It seemed to be laughing at me. I pushed the thought away.

Life returned just as I was laying Samuel out on the bed, making sure his limbs were straight and his eyes were closed. She took one look at him then made a sound in the back of her throat that sounded rather a lot like disgust. "Stars, Cal, you killed him."

I straightened Samuel's shirt cuffs. "I am unsure as to why you are surprised. It is, after all, what I am meant to do while your husband is on holiday."

Life pulled me away from the body, flicking a disinterested glance at it over her shoulder. Now that Samuel was dead, I don't think that Life actually cared what became of his body. There wasn't much in it for her. She did grab me by the collar and shove me into the chair where I had recovered from dying before. I tugged at my own shirt and suit jacket. It was ruined—bleeding out will do that—but it was the principle of the thing.

"What about the boon?" Life demanded, folding her arms. "You shouldn't have killed him before—"

"He asked me to make it quick," I said. My voice had gone back to the flat, empty sound that happened whenever my emotions were pushed to the side. Whatever was happening to me—whether I was actually fluctuating between logic and emotion—I didn't want to fathom; I grabbed onto the static calm with veracity. "Do you think I'm stupid enough to have killed him without fulfilling the boon?"

"You are extremely ignorant in the matters of Elsewhere," Life retorted, pacing around the tiny house. She threw up her hands. "Did you even think to *offer* him life?"

"We both assumed, rightly, I imagine, that you would not offer him again the same vitality that you had before. The same extension to his life. The alternative would have meant him walking around in the state you left him: weak, exhausted, barely able to move, his soul stronger than his lifeforce." I wondered how long I would have to sit here and discuss this before Life took me back to Elsewhere. If she didn't, I would have to find another way. That would mean hiking down this mountain, finding a phone, calling Yolanda—back in Elsewhere, mind you—and figuring out a means of transport across realms. I would likely not return to

Elsewhere before Death got back from his holiday in the tropics.

Life glared at me. "So?"

Well… that alternative hadn't occurred to me. "So?" I asked. "So, you would prefer your champion to wander around in staggering amounts of pain, with no purpose now that his family is gone, no money, no resources of any kind. He would barely make it to the bottom of the mountain before collapsing. Then what? Would you have him lay there, his body decomposing while his soul stayed tethered to it?"

Life raised a single shoulder, her expression cold. "If he were a true champion of mine, he would have fought for me."

I opened my mouth to argue. I wanted to demand to know how she could be so callous, how she could be so self-serving, nearsighted and cruel. Then, I remembered just who it was that I was talking with and realised that arguing would be pointless. Life, for all her faults and assets, would never be able to understand what it was that made us humans—even other "lesser beings" who were powerful enough to rule Elsewhere—do what we did.

That was, after all, why I had bargained with Life *and* Death back in 1494 to leave us to our own devices, as much as possible. This was why they weren't allowed to get directly involved anymore.

Because neither of them, no matter how much a person could hope otherwise, understood.

"Well, it is done," was all I said. I rose from the

chair. "I believe I have fulfilled the task that you needed of me. Can we get back to Elsewhere, now?"

Life pouted. She actually stuck out her bottom lip and blinked petulant eyes at me. "Oh, come on, Cal, there's still so much to do! We haven't even got to see the seven wonders of the world. Or we could go see how Jahanara gets on with the Fae—I'm afraid I left her at the edge of their territory without anything so much as an introduction. Or we could—"

I held up a hand and replied with a grimace. "No. I don't work for you, Life. Neither am I your champion. You asked for my help in collecting the soul of your champion. Well, I've done it. Now, fulfil your obligation and return me to my office."

"My husband's office, you mean," Life said, a smooth smile dancing over her features. There was mischief there. She seemed completely unconcerned with the fact that I had refused her offer, again. "I found you in my husband's office, not your own."

I sighed; did such things really matter right now? Maybe they did. "Fine. Just take me back."

Life tilted her head, tapped her mouth with a finger, then smiled brightly and said, "No."

With a flare of light, she was gone and I was left in the house with a body.

Figures.

As it turns out, people look at you oddly when you trek down a mountain wearing a bloody, ruined suit and Italian leather shoes. They especially look at you oddly when that whole village is meant to be abandoned, a place left to the spirits who took Jahanara and then brought her back. Then, when I spoke perfect, Oxford English, the people in the closest inhabited village all but screamed and ran away.

I did manage to hitch a ride with an irreverent man who was heading to Jaipur to see if he could make his fortune. His English was terrible, my Hindi was nonexistent, but we seemed to get along well enough. It helped that he had an old CD player in his car and a seemingly endless collection of Beatles albums.

Several hundred hours later—I exaggerate, but there are only so many times you can listen to The White Album without going crazy—we arrived in Jaipur. It was a bustling town that, luckily, didn't seem to care too much about my ruined clothes or my lack of phone and wallet. I managed to beg a phone call off of a woman who was running a store carrying all sorts of spices.

Amazingly, Yolanda actually answered her phone.

"Cal Thorpe Marketing Services," she said cheerily, "this is Yolanda the rock troll. How may I help you?"

"Mentioning that you are a rock troll is irrelevant," I said, apparently in a strange enough state of mind that I couldn't even say "hello".

"Cal!" Yolanda practically shouted through the

phone. I had to hold it away from my ear and bob a smile at the shop owner, who was watching me through narrowed eyes. A customer walked in and she turned to deal with him. "You are not missing forever! We came to work and there was a note from Death about going on holiday, but you were not there and we did not know whether Death had taken you on holiday or made you disappear for being insupportinative or something."

"Insupp—you mean insubordinate? No, that wasn't what happened," I said. I looked around and lowered my voice, not knowing quite how much English the shop owner actually understood. "Death made me his proxy and I have been out dealing with the collection of a particularly difficult soul. But I'm stuck in the mortal realms. In Jaipur."

I decided not to mention Life, or the strangeness I had experienced with my own mental state. All of that could wait until I was back in the office and feeling less… sordid.

"Oh, okay!" Yolanda said. I could practically hear her grinning; she probably thought this was all a fun adventure or something. My assistant seemed to fluctuate between two extremes: happy and terrified. Today was a happy day. "I'll call up a wyvern and see if you can't be picked up or something."

"I thought wyverns couldn't cross realm boundaries," I said. Now, a dragon could do whatever they wanted, but their less intelligent and distantly related cousins were not nearly so capable. Not to mention that getting a dragon to offer such services willingly would be nigh impossible. And I'd never actually met a dragon, just heard rumours. "Perhaps you can contact Iggy, instead."

Yggdral was Death's wraith chauffeur, a fairly quiet and intense chap who happened to drive one of the most stunning pieces of machinery I'd ever seen: a 1920s Rolls Royce Silver Phantom.

He was also exclusively Death's chauffeur.

"I don't know, Cal," Yolanda said, the hesitation in her voice moving her away from her "happy" state. I sighed.

"I'm acting as Death's proxy. I have a goodly number of his powers right now. Perhaps you could just call and *ask* Iggy if he'd be willing to help me out. Unless you have a better means of getting back to Elsewhere?" By now, I was feeling irritation rise up in the back of my mind. It was getting harder and harder to push the emotions away and I didn't even know how genuine they were. They *felt* genuine, but then, they had felt almost false when I had someone else's soul running through me. I just didn't know.

And that terrified me.

"Okay, Cal," Yolanda said. Without further preamble—or an alternate means of travel—she hung up. I replaced the receiver, gave my effusive English thanks to the shop owner, who nodded kindly at me but who also followed me with sharkish eyes, and then went out to the street.

Yolanda, thank goodness, didn't let me down. A few minutes later, the Rolls appeared in the street, engine purring like a panther, metal gleaming and seemingly impervious to the dust and smog of the air. The locals just walked around it as though it weren't there, though I did notice a few people who managed to see it and eyed it appreciatively. I gathered that those were the local magical beings.

I slid into the back of the car and Iggy fixed me with a firm glare, the twin points of blue flame that served as his eyes making that particular expression all the more intense. I waved halfheartedly. "Thank you for doing this. Life… asked me for my help, as I'm Death's proxy, then abandoned me here when it was all done."

Iggy, as usual, didn't say anything, but turned his attention to the road in front of him and began driving off. I was unsure if he could actually speak, or if he just preferred not to, but the silence was very pleasant. I could feel a creeping exhaustion slithering over my shoulders and wrapping itself around my throat. I could manage quite a lot without a soul, but I had been up for what felt like several days, died multiple times, and dealt with Life. I closed my eyes before the last vestiges of the mortal realm slipped away outside the car windows.

I opened them again when the motion of the car stopped and found myself in the familiar drive of my little house and office building on Death's property. I slid out of the car. "Thank you," I said, but Iggy was already driving away.

Yolanda and Agravane appeared in the doorway to the offices on the lower floor of my building. Yolanda was grinning widely at me, her extraordinarily bright teeth a beacon of joy. Agravane, by comparison, was looking particularly grumpy. He wasn't scowling, but there was little that could do battle with Yolanda's joy and come out looking cheerful.

"You're back! And you're not gone!" Yolanda leaped forwards and wrapped her arms around me, squeezing me into lung paroxysms. Given that she was built like a tank, this didn't take more than a second or so. Then, she caught a whiff of my suit, wrinkled her nose and dropped me. "You are covered in blood."

"Most of it's mine," I assured her.

Agravane snorted.

"I'm sure I have rather a lot to catch up on, but I would very much appreciate a shower and perhaps some sleep. My body seems to be run down," I said, that comforting coolness back. Yolanda agreed immediately and skipped away inside, leaving me to walk beside Agravane.

"There has been a lot of coffee appearing in the cupboards," he said, watching me for a reaction.

I paused, feeling true joy spill over until I was practically beaming. "I met a brownie," I said, pushing my way into the building so that I could hunt out some coffee. "I agreed to do her marketing for some coffee. Apparently there was more coffee involved in the bargain than I anticipated."

Agravane nodded, seemingly pleased with my answer. But before I could steer myself towards the coffee and bury my palate in that delightful beverage, Agravane pushed me towards the stairs that led to my apartments. I grumbled, but acquiesced.

In discarding my suit as I prepared the hottest

shower I could manage, I found the crumpled up set of instructions from Death, informing me of what my duties were. It was illogical of me to try to hold on to them; they were stained with my blood, falling to pieces and, besides, I already knew what it was that I was meant to do. As I threw them into the trash, however, the last page fluttered before my eyes and I snatched it out of the air.

There, on the last line of the last page, was text written in all capitals:

DO NOT AGREE TO HELP LIFE WITH ANY FAVOURS.

Well. Now he tells me.

A MERCIFUL DEATH

"Y ou're looking rather the worse for wear."

I looked up from where I was sitting at Death's desk in his office—it was quieter there than in my own office, where Agravane and Yolanda were gallivanting about doing marketing business, business I actually wanted to be doing. Death was standing in the entrance to the room, wearing another neatly pressed three-piece white linen suit, a sea blue pocket square, a cane with a decorative silver head, a Panama hat, and a cravat with a hibiscus tie stick stabbed into it. He looked well rested and pleased, precisely how you should look after a nice holiday.

I, on the other hand, had purposely avoided looking in the mirror for the last two days so that I wouldn't have to see the reality staring me in the face. I had lost weight, had shadows under my eyes that looked almost as dark as the ones that were following me around, bore a distinct tremor that only seemed to go away when I was focusing on the orb to collect souls, and couldn't get enough coffee in my system to combat the fatigue I was feeling.

"You're back," I said, feeling the urgent need to state the obvious.

"Indeed," Death said, depositing his suitcase neatly inside the door. "I see the world hasn't fallen to pieces since I've been away."

"No, it hasn't fallen to pieces." Another unnecessary statement, but I think somewhere between my brain and my mouth, Life had got in the way. I hadn't seen her since she left me in the Himalayas, but the aftereffects lingered in my mind. I had lost all sense of logic or illogic, emotion or emptiness. And her offer kept whispering through my thoughts when I least wanted it, promising freedom from this uncertainty, a stable condition.

Death swept forwards, sitting in the chair opposite me and deftly crossed an ankle over his knee. He fixed me with a serious gaze, the voids that were his eyes feeling far friendlier than what I had endured over the last week or so.

Three more times had I delved into the orb, collecting souls en masse and dying for my efforts. Each time I did so, the craving grew stronger and I could barely function until it was again time for me to reach out and collect souls. The number of people I had touched to end their lives and released their souls was beyond calculation and yet I felt no sorrow for them, only the need to keep going.

I reached out and practically pushed the orb, now glowing yellow with collected souls, towards Death.

"Take it," I rasped, barely able to keep from snatching it back.

Death did, regarding the orb with a curious expression. "Interesting," he said, a quiet murmur.

"Interesting?" I snapped. "How, pray tell?"

"You do not seem so steeped in logic alternating with emotion. Tell me, do you think your condition has stabilised at all?" Death asked with what sounded to me like mild curiosity. He didn't seem inclined to answer my question at all. I curled my lip.

"Stabilised?" I asked, voice cracking. "Do I *look* stabilised to you?"

"Indeed not."

I took a deep breath, fluctuating between fury and despair and emptiness. I couldn't regulate anything and I couldn't push emotions away. "What's interesting?" I asked again, clenching my hands into fists to keep them from shaking.

"You're the first proxy I've utilised to actually collect more than a handful of souls," Death said, holding the orb up as though he could see each and every soul I had gathered with nothing more than a glance. He lowered the orb and looked at me again. "You should not have been able to do that."

I allowed myself to gape for a full ten seconds. When I say "allow", I mean I had absolutely no control over whether I gaped or didn't. I collected my thoughts and swallowed. "You left me *instructions*," I said. I was pushing myself out of the chair before I could stop myself. "I just followed them!"

Death rose also, considerably more gracefully, his

manner more elegant and his expression far more intimidating. "And yet the matter remains, Cal, that it should not have been done." He still sounded nothing more than mildly curious. As if this whole experience was just a bird outside the window: pretty, a quick distraction, soon forgotten.

I exploded into rage. Just as had happened with the Iron witch, Death's own shadows writhed around me, moving in time with my anger and acting out my will. I lunged around the desk, reaching for Death. Had I been thinking rationally—had I an *ounce* of logic when fuelled by emotion—I would have realised what a stupid action it was. Instead, I managed to get within a foot of Death before he acted, as calmly and reasonably as ever.

He touched me on my forehead.

The powers that had been his left me, a vacuum sucking out air and leaving a vast nothingness in its place. The shadows retreated into his darker-than-dark skin. The assured inevitability that I carried at my centre vanished, replaced with a slightly nauseous sensation. I collapsed into the chair that Death had just occupied, gasping and panting as my body adjusted its equilibrium to what had just happened.

Death had retaken his loaned powers. He hadn't warned me, he hadn't said a single word, he just took them away. And left the indefatigable craving for a soul behind.

I was whimpering and crying when I came to my senses. Death had taken my seat on the other side of the desk, the orb sitting neatly to one side like a paperweight. He folded his fingers together and leaned forwards. "Do you feel better?" he asked.

"No," I said. I didn't, either. I didn't feel like I was going to drown in a sea of uncontrollable feeling, but neither did I think I was anywhere near stable. The craving seemed to have replaced any sureness I felt about what I was doing. The last few days were nothing but pure hubris in my mind compared with the insignificant ink stain that I was, now. "Yes," I said a moment later.

I sat up, physical tinglings reminding me of the stress I had been placing on my body recently. Soulless or not, there were limits and once again I seemed to have reached mine. "What is happening to me?" I asked.

"I am unsure," Death replied. That was bound to make a person brim with confidence. "Perhaps if you describe the last ten days, explaining how you managed to do what you did and what you experienced, I can form a better conclusion."

I straightened my tie even as I shuffled my feet on the rug beneath my chair. I nodded. "I followed all your instructions, except one…"

I don't know how long it took to explain my most recent adventures, if you will, to Death. I do know that by the time I was done, tea had been placed on the desk between us and I somehow had managed to eat three sandwiches and a tiny pile of macaroons. I finished my descriptions with the cravings, holding out my still-shaking hands as proof.

Then, silence.

Death leaned back in his chair, the leather creaking as he did so. He steepled his fingers before his face, empty eyes staring straight at me and yet not looking in my direction. I waited. "Hmm," Death said after a moment.

That was it?

I opened my mouth to ask as much when Death held up a single hand, preventing me from speaking.

"Once again, Cal Thorpe, you do not seem to adhere to any of my expectations. There are two things that I find particularly interesting in your tale. Well, three, but a discussion of my wife and her motivations is not what I want at this moment." Death lifted a finger. "One: the fact that you could collect souls on a massive scale, connecting with people as they were dying no matter where you were and where they were. You say it simply took a matter of focus with the orb as a centre, but I have never met a being other than myself—and one or two notable exceptions, which I shall explain shortly—that can do such a thing. Two: the fact that you managed to gather people's souls while they were still, technically alive."

"They were very nearly dead," I pointed out. "The Instant of Death, like when you found me."

Death tilted his head, smiled thinly and said, "Not quite. You should have, with the abilities I gave you, only managed to collect a person's soul *after* they were already dead. If you had reached a person in the Instant of Death, then yes, you would have been able to collect it then, but the likelihood of you doing that on a large scale or even more than once is statistically unlikely. I simply did not give you that power."

I shrank into my chair, not quite certain if I wanted to hear what Death was going to say, next. Turns out, I didn't.

Death leaned forwards and placed his hands flat on his desk, his expression one of interest and sympathy. That sent shivers up my spine, though no corresponding emotion rose to the surface. "The fact of the matter is, Cal, that you collected people's souls just before they died. You did not collect them *after* they died, nor did you collect but a few as they reached the Instant of Death. You collected them before. Which means that you killed them."

When you hear news like that, you expect to have a moment where all you can hear is your heart beating in your ears. You expect to black out for a moment, to have the world fall away until the words can grasp onto some sort of solid truth and settle inside you, where you can either accept them or deny them. You don't expect to just sit there, the only sound the quiet crackle of the fire place or the ticking of the clock.

"I… what?" I said, my voice strangely steady.

"You killed them." Death nodded gently then sighed, still with that slight smile. "You did not murder them; they were meant to die at any moment in any case. But you were the direct cause of their death. You released their soul from their body before the body died. Even as you did with Samuel Phipps, when you saw that releasing his soul would kill him. It is, once again, an ability that I did not give you."

"I… killed those people?" My voice was quieter now.

Death nodded. "It is nothing to feel guilt over, Cal. They would have died in any case. They would even have died more violent, painful deaths than what you provided. It is, truthfully, what I would have done."

"But—"

"You are not hearing what I'm saying. It was not a wrong that you did. Quite the opposite, in fact. But it should have been impossible." Death was now leaning far over his desk, staring vividly at me. That slight smile was wider, as if he were *pleased* with what I'd done. What monstrosities I'd committed.

My vision wobbled slightly. When it focused again, Death was nearly grinning.

"Now, there are beings out there who have such abilities. Whose calling lines up with my own duties, who have in past acted as my assistants and deputies in ruling the Lands of Silence. I believe you may be one of them, though I haven't seen one in many centuries. Not since, well, let me think now. Not since the plagues broke out across Europe the last time, I think." Death nodded, drumming his fingers on the desk as he remembered.

This was it. This was what Life had been insinuating when she whispered in my ear. This was what the witch had known, what Samuel had taken advantage of in binding me. I might have been human once, but I wasn't human, now. Death had made me into something else, either intentionally or otherwise. Now I was a killer, a murderer, an addict always looking for the next fix.

"You're a Reaper, Cal," Death said. He stood and walked around the desk, holding his arms wide as if to wrap me in a hug. "A Grim Reaper."

I lunged for the waste bin and vomited the sandwich and macaroons into it. Death patted my back and I could have sworn that I felt the touch of his power even through my suit jacket. When I was done emptying my stomach, I pulled away from him with a strangled cry and fled his office.

I only looked back once.

I had never run through Elsewhere before. I had travelled around it by wyvern, by vampire kidnapping, by chauffeur, but I had never run through it before. I had always been content to remain —unless out on assignment—in Death's lands, saturated with blues and greys and silvers, a land of peace and mist and quiet. Now, I ran past Death's borders without a second thought, ignoring the fact that I was likely ruining another pair of shoes.

I had no intention of running forever, but for the moment I needed to get away, to forget the words that Death had just told me.

Killer.

Murderer.

Reaper.

Ender of lives.

I didn't know what a Reaper was apart from the stories. I'd always thought it *was* Death, another one of his guises, not an entirely separate creature from the same domain. Similar abilities to Death. Beings that could *kill* a person with a touch and release their soul. Maybe they couldn't take the souls to wherever they were meant to go, but even that was enough to have bile rising in my throat again.

I was running on pure emotion now, everything unfiltered and raw, vying for my attention. Memories flashed through my head, reminding me of every single person I had killed. The old woman, the dying punk, that *girl*. I knew that death and dying was an inevitable part of everyone's lives, that it wasn't anything to fear, but it was something entirely different when *I* was the one doing the killing.

I was a marketing and public relations specialist, for crying out loud! I excelled at building people up, at making them important, influential. I did my best to help present a smooth, consistent, magnificent image to the world at large. I was really, really good at my job. And now that was completely overshadowed by the fact that I was neither human, nor a good guy.

Not anymore.

I didn't stop running through Elsewhere, breathing in the saturated colours of the world beyond Death's realm. I watched tree folk and river folk argue on the bank of a stream. I watched ogres stumbling out of a tavern. I watched a car pull up and release a bunch of giggling satyrs. None of them noticed me. Or, if they did, then they made a point to look away.

I kept running.

My shoes were ruined by now and breath was ragged in my lungs. I was fairly certain that I had already exceeded my body's limits earlier that morning, before Death's return. Now, I was just being stupid. I didn't care at all.

At the edge of my vision, a ridiculously garish palace rose from the ground. It was exceptionally well built, with wings and turrets and a garden that would have put any botanical landscape in the mortal realms to shame. I turned towards the house, my feet slamming onto the ground, slipping slightly on the gravel drive as I did so.

Even from a distance, I could hear the party that was going on inside as if I were in the midst of it already. Music pounded out through the grounds, some mix of 1920s jazz and modern rock-and-roll, the combination somehow acceptable and even really good. People of all sorts stumbled about in varying costumes: nymphs with vibrant green skin, beings that looked like they were made of stone, tiny goblins, elves, faeries, trolls, vampires, you name it. Many of them carried drinks. Even more of them were dancing, shouting their appreciation of life to the skies.

I ran past them and into the house without a hitch in my step. I had been here before; I knew my way.

The palatial house was set up with a hundred different rooms, all sporting some sort of dancing or music or games or just conversation. Each room had someone in it, mostly many someones. They were, generally, incoherent and drunk, not necessarily on alcohol. Everyone here was smiling, happy to be here, well aware of the fleeting permanence of this moment.

Frankly, it was like watching *The Great Gatsby*, except all the characters were magical beings.

This was Life's house.

I pushed past people, ignoring shouts of alarm and interest alike. I pushed aside two drinks that were thrust randomly in my direction. I nearly vomited again when a plate of sandwiches passed in front of me, bringing Death's words to the forefront of my mind. Some sweet-smelling smoke wafted towards me as I stumbled my way up the stairs towards the back of the house. Immediately, my mind began to spin.

I barely managed to get one foot in front of the other by the time I reached the back of the house. I pushed open a set of grand, wooden doors, their hinges completely silent and smooth. Once the doors were open, I practically fell into the room, my stumbling quickly turning into a true trip. I landed on my knees, my hands bracing myself on the floor. A moment later, even that came up to meet me and I greeted it gladly.

The doors closed silently behind me as I lay on the floor, the world spinning around me in a myriad of colours that was so desperately like Life herself. I closed my eyes, grateful for the silence that now permeated the air.

"Well, well, isn't this a surprise?"

I opened my eyes to find that the world had stopped spinning, and that Life stood over me, a smirk painting her features. I pushed myself to my feet, slowly, and let out a groan. Everything hurt in a way that it shouldn't have done after a simple run. Not that I was terribly *good* at running, but it shouldn't have made my elbows scream in agony.

I looked around the grand hallway and quickly averted my eyes as they passed over portraits of people I knew. Charlotte the Unkillable, the half-giantess I had known in 1494, scowled down at me from a frame, her massive greatsword held in her hands as though she would leap down and strike at me. I wondered what she would think of all of this. Then there was Magnus, the jewel thief whose murder I had investigated. And Samuel Phipps, his portrait showing him as a much younger, stronger man, a gleam of pride in his eyes.

This was the gallery of Life's champions, many of them centuries, even millennia old. I hadn't ever seen all the portraits there. I wasn't sure I wanted to.

"This is the point where you tell me why you're here, Cal," Life said, stepping forwards and brushing a finger over the frame with a picture of a woman I didn't recognise.

"Can't you guess?" I asked, sounding at least a little more normal. I didn't feel like I was going to scream, that is.

Life bared her teeth in a feral smile. "Oh, I can guess, but it's far more satisfying if you say it."

"Death told me what I am… what I'm becoming," I said. I ground my teeth together as Life just stood there, smiling ferociously. She was truly enjoying this. "He says I'm becoming a Grim Reaper."

She cackled, throwing her head back and making her ever-changing hair sway in the air. I felt my stomach drop, though I don't know why. "And you've come here to see if I can change you back? Well, let me tell you, Cal, I can't. There is no going back, not now!"

She didn't have to sound so gleeful about it.

"I know." I pressed my mouth together, wondering if I would regret the words even as I spoke them. But still, I spoke them: "I want to accept your offer. To work for you. In exchange for stabilising my condition."

Her eyes, just as arresting as Death's deep voids, flashed to mine and suddenly the grin she was wearing wasn't so much ferocious as victorious. I knew I was probably making a mistake. I had never trusted Life, not from the moment that I met her and she tried to draw me in and potentially kill me, just out of curiosity. I'd had my fair share of run-ins with her, too. Times when she was fickle and dangerous just for the sake of it. This last week hadn't changed my opinion of her at all.

But now, I was just as mistrustful of my employer. Death was, and had been, extremely powerful and terrifying. I'd never wondered if he intended to hurt me, to change me, to make me something horrible and cruel.

Life stepped up to me, so close that she was a hair's breadth away from touching her nose to mine. I was getting cross-eyed just from trying to look at her. "You would be my errand boy," she decided, running a finger down my cheek. "A gofer."

"Okay," I said, ready to accept whatever demeaning job she threw my direction. "I'd still… I'd still have to work for Death. I've made an agreement."

Life waved a dismissive hand. "Of course! I'm not stupid, Cal."

"Right." I didn't know what else to say, but some sort of burden had been lifted from my shoulders. "Um… do I have to sign a contract or something?"

"Or something," Life said. She surged forwards too fast for me to follow and pressed up against me, kissing me with abandon. I squeaked in the back of my throat before the true seductive temptation of what was happening to me hit. Then, I kissed her back. Hard.

We came up for air some short time later. Life was still smiling that fox-smile, and I felt like my brain had been mauled. It wasn't quite the same overwhelming force that had taken me when I agreed to work for Death, but there was definitely a sensation of binding, a knowledge that I owed her a duty, too. Nothing near as strong as what I owed Death. I noticed it, though.

"Welcome to the team, Cal," Life said. She put her hands on my shoulders and turned me to face the gallery wall. I was suddenly staring straight at a portrait of myself. I looked… powerful. Imposing. Grand. And, in the depth of my eyes behind my glasses, I looked frightened.

Oh, yeah. This was *definitely* a bad idea.

ACKNOWLEDGMENTS

As always, writing a book is a journey that involves many hands.

Thank you always to my readers, who have come this far in a series that tries not to take itself too seriously. I appreciate every one of you.

A special thanks to Fay, who designed this cover and made me snort-laugh with that perfect picture of Death in a cheesy tourist shirt. Your covers always amaze.

Thank you also to my dad, who listens to all of my ideas and then encourages me to take them that extra step into the world of weird. And for having me watch Death Takes a Holiday, which is absolutely nothing like this book.

ABOUT THE AUTHOR

E.G. Stone is an independent author who has been writing, creating and causing vast amounts of trouble since the age of six. Since then, E.G. has improved rather a lot in both the trouble-causing and writing and now spends her time writing fantasy and science fiction. When not writing, she is off musing about the workings of languages, both real and created, or drawing and sewing. E.G. reads voraciously, perhaps to the point of slight-insanity. Weird, nerdy, perhaps a little crazy, she is having a grand old time writing, reading, reviewing, interviewing, and, naturally, continuing her endeavours in causing trouble.

ALSO BY E.G. STONE

Speaker of Words

The Crow and the King

The Wing Cycle:
The One Who Could Not Fly
To Never Hear the Song
The Forsaking of the Blind

On Behalf of Death:
The Innocence of Death
Knowledge Aforethought
A Party of Certainties
When Death's Away
Mischief, Mayhem, and Shakespeare
The Long Way Home

www.ingramcontent.com/pod-product-compliance
Lightning Source LLC
Chambersburg PA
CBHW021328190726
48288CB00003B/1005